Here was the

His brown eyes sparkled h
this dance, Miss Windhave.

She'd fooled him, too. He didn't recognize her behind the mask.

My, he was bold in how he stared. With the stranger this close, she hesitated. She was accustomed to protecting herself in this crime-ridden town. "I don't believe I know you, sir."

"That's what a masquerade is all about. Come."

Just like that. A command. He locked his fingers around her wrist and marched her past the dance floor and onto the balcony. He leaned against a stone wall, and she was trapped.

The stranger's riveting gaze made her tense. There was a black glint of trouble in his eyes.

Sensing danger, she leaped to run, but it was too late. He called to two men hidden in shadow. She kicked and bit. They shoved a kerchief into her mouth.

What did he want from her?

* * *

Wanted in Alaska
Harlequin® Historical #931—February 2009

Praise for Kate Bridges

KLONDIKE FEVER

"Humor, sensuality and high adventure."
—*Romantic Times BOOKreviews*

KLONDIKE WEDDING

"Likable characters and an engaging storyline that keeps the reader entranced the whole way through."
—*Romance Junkies*

KLONDIKE DOCTOR

"Her heroes are the strong, silent type, and it's simply delightful to watch them fall in love with her headstrong heroines. Not only is the romance wonderful, the unique backdrop adds another fascinating dimension to a terrific story."
—*Romantic Times BOOKreviews*

THE COMMANDER

"Bridges' poignant, tender romance goes straight for the heart with its deep emotions and beautiful message of redemption and love's healing powers."
—*Romantic Times BOOKreviews*

THE PROPOSITION

"Bridges displays her talent for creating a story of great emotional depth."
—*Romantic Times BOOKreviews*

"The latest in Bridges' Canadian Mounted Police series is beautifully set against the natural grandeur of the Rockies and provides more pleasure for readers who like Western historicals that deftly mix danger and desire."
—*Booklist*

LUKE'S RUNAWAY BRIDE

"Bridges is comfortable in her Western setting, and her characters' humorous sparring make this boisterous mix of romance and skullduggery an engrossing read."
—*Publishers Weekly*

KATE BRIDGES

Wanted in Alaska

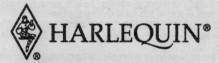

HARLEQUIN®

TORONTO • NEW YORK • LONDON
AMSTERDAM • PARIS • SYDNEY • HAMBURG
STOCKHOLM • ATHENS • TOKYO • MILAN • MADRID
PRAGUE • WARSAW • BUDAPEST • AUCKLAND

Recycling programs
for this product may
not exist in your area.

ISBN-13: 978-0-373-29531-9
ISBN-10:   0-373-29531-6

WANTED IN ALASKA

Copyright © 2009 by Katherine Haupt

www.eHarlequin.com

Printed in U.S.A.

This book is dedicated to my husband, Greg,
and daughter, Samantha, with much love. Our trip to
Alaska to research this book is one I'll always remember.

Chapter One

Skagway, District of Alaska
Early June 1899

He was a tough man to ignore. And he kept looking her way.

Miss Autumn MacNeil tried to come up with a name for the man with the penetrating brown eyes, but couldn't place him. Was he someone from a recent audience who'd heard her sing?

"You have a new admirer," Victoria Windhaven whispered as they stood on the stairs overlooking the crowded dance floor of the grand ballroom.

"Perhaps it's you he's focused on," said Autumn.

"It's definitely you."

Dressed in black tails, elegant wool pants, a blue silk cravat and a spotless cream shirt that accentuated the intensity of his dark face, he'd walked into the masquerade ball at the Imperial Hotel shortly after eight. He'd tapped an older gent on the shoulder, appeared to ask a question, then both men had turned and stared at Autumn.

Autumn glanced away but her pulse strummed with excitement. Her lashes flicked against the velvet mask that covered her eyes. Such fun, after such a long winter. It felt exhilarating to be fooling everyone on this splendid Saturday evening. Even him.

The bustle of activity around them flushed her with heat. Beneath her tight corset and the borrowed, ivory lace blouse that covered every inch of flesh from her chin to her bosom, her stomach tingled with anticipation. Even the pins in her brown wig yanked at her roots, heightening her senses.

Autumn moved her toes in time to the music and admired everyone dressed in such top form tonight. "Since I'm masquerading as you, who do you suppose he thinks he's staring at?"

Victoria smiled and shrugged beneath her blond wig. "At least I don't have to *sing* as you tonight. That would give me away immediately."

Pretending to be each other had been Autumn's idea. There'd be a prize for best costume, and they had agreed if either of them won, they'd donate half of the generous fifty dollars to Skagway's charity drive to build a proper hospital.

The orchestra began the Viennese Waltz. Autumn couldn't resist humming as couples on the polished pine floor practiced twirl after twirl.

Victoria, one of the town's three precious nurses, looked sinful in the low-cut black velvet costume Autumn had lent her. Who would've known they would become such close friends on the sea voyage to Alaska, twelve months ago, when both had nearly died of loneliness? In Seattle, before Autumn had left to seek her fortune, she had lost her grandparents, one shortly after the other. For the first time in her life, she was totally alone.

Trying to ignore the pang of grief that often arose without her control, Autumn raised her fan to her heated face and waved it madly. She'd concentrate on more joyful events this evening. She was waiting for her dance partners to arrive. Surely they'd be here soon. How fortunate she was that things might finally be coming together in her life…. Well, almost.

Autumn spotted her employer, Mr. Kennedy, across the ballroom and this evoked another type of sentiment. Apprehension. She nudged her friend. "I need to speak with him."

"Good luck," Victoria hollered behind her. "Don't give in!"

Autumn's red suede skirt shifted around her high buckled boots. She pressed a hand to the black leather belt cinched at her waist and maneuvered past the ball gowns, cravats and Stetsons.

She felt the stranger's eyes upon her, but she ignored him.

"Evenin', Miss Windhaven," said the town's clockmaker as she dipped by, mistaking her for her friend. "Thank you for that liniment. Rash is nearly gone."

Autumn smiled but said nothing to correct him.

"Miss Windhaven," called another in error. "Save me a dance!"

"Me, too," said Deputy Marshal Brander as she passed. He pressed his thick arms against his chest, adding with bold accuracy, "Miss MacNeil."

The directness of his gaze made her pulse jump. The lawman had recognized her. But she ignored him, too, and latched on to the bulky elbow of her target. "Mr. Kennedy, a word, please."

The man swung around, his false beard for the evening looking ridiculously out of place on his usually clean-shaven face. "Miss MacNeil—" He'd recognized her voice, but stopped himself when he saw her in the wig and mask. "Or is it Miss Windhaven?"

"Right the first time," she said in a cheerful tone. "Autumn."

"How did your meeting go yesterday with the banker?"

A sticky warmth infused her face. "Not so well… He…"

"Turned you down, too?"

"Yes, sir, but I've come to ask you. Please don't sell the hotel. I've got an appointment with the manager of the credit and loan—"

"You say this every time."

"He seems very amenable to my skills as a bookkeeper."

"I told you. The gentlemen who made me that offer want an answer within the next day."

"My appointment, sir, is on Monday. Surely you can let any business dealings rest on the Sabbath."

Mr. Kennedy pursed his lips and gazed around the room, as if trying to come to terms with something. "You're a woman. No one is going to lend you any money, my dear."

She swayed. Then took a deep breath.

"You're pretty and you have a nice voice. Accept what you do best."

"What I do best, Mr. Kennedy, is balancing a ledger. The shop I ran with my grandparents—"

"If you were so good with that shop, why aren't you still running it?"

She stung from the comment. Her stomach quivered as she fought for words. "My grandpa was a lithographer. The sole artist for the shop. When he passed away, my grandma and I had nothing left to sell."

An artist, just as she was with her voice. Something she would never again rest her entire future on. Running this hotel—with its gift shop, restaurant and twenty-eight rooms—was something much more dependable. Her grandmother, may God rest her soul, would agree with Autumn's dream. The two of them together had barely survived in Seattle after Grandpa had succumbed to pneumonia.

"There's nothing I can—"

"Mr. Kennedy." Autumn pressed a hand on his prickly wool sleeve. Confidence attracted confidence, and so she kept her manner firm. "You have three young daughters of your own. At some point in their lives, they will come to you and ask for something you feel is equally outrageous. Perhaps one of them will want to own a hotel, as well. Three days. Just give me three more days."

He stared into her face and said nothing. But the longer he was silent, the more hopeful she became. He wasn't saying no.

With a quirk of his scraggly beard, he nodded and left.

The pressure in her chest subsided. Roughly ten percent of Skagway's population was made up of women, the numbers were climbing and some of them were doing quite well as shop owners. Others had staked claims in the Klondike and were just as rich as their male counterparts. Still, it wasn't fair that most bankers thought men were smarter and worked harder in business than women.

There was a tiny thread of optimism here. That's all she needed. The same thread of optimism she'd felt two months after her grandma's funeral in Seattle. As far as Autumn had been concerned, she'd had three choices there: accept the marriage proposal from her grandpa's solicitor, thirty years her senior. Stay in Seattle and work as a housemaid to pay her bills. Or take the next ship to Alaska and get hired as a singer through the advertisement she'd read in *Skagway News*. Until she saw an opening in a business venture, something much more solid than singing.

Someone tapped her waist from behind. It had to be one of her dance partners. Breathless, she wheeled around, craning her neck upward, expecting to see a familiar face.

Instead, here was the mysterious stranger.

There went her stomach again.

His brown eyes sparkled beneath the candlelit chandelier. A man well into his thirties. "May I have this dance, Miss Windhaven?"

Yes, she'd fooled him, too.

My, he was bold in how he stared. Autumn squirmed in her red lace corset. Not *everything* she wore was borrowed. Not her underclothes.

With the stranger this close, she hesitated. Sometimes, men who listened to her sing got carried away with their feelings. She was accustomed to protecting herself, onstage and off, particularly in this crime-ridden town, and thus responded, "I don't believe I know you, sir."

"That's what a masquerade is all about."

"But…but I do recognize the other gentlemen who've asked for my time, and I don't seem—"

"Perhaps the other men are bores."

She shifted her weight. "I beg your pardon?"

"You were tapping your toes and sipping your punch with great restraint. Perhaps it's better, more adventurous, if you don't know my name."

"Ah…huh…" Who was this man with such rude manners? "I peg you as a politician."

A hint of humor tugged at his dark cheeks. His eyes remained unreadable. "Not so."

"Then perhaps someone who does dramatic readings on stage?"

He tilted his dark head. His hair was neatly trimmed, his silky skin patted with barber's lotions, the lightest scent of mint. "You think me quite boisterous. Aim for something more obscure."

"Well, I have heard the town hired a new coffin maker."

His lips lifted with definite amusement. "I'd be too lonely. No one to talk to all day."

"You could talk to the dead. Perhaps *they* wouldn't mind if your manner was a little brisk."

"I apologize for my briskness. May I have this dance?"

"It's nearly over now. Sadly, you've talked your way through it."

From behind, a large warm hand cupped hers. A different man. She turned to see Shaun, owner of the town's largest bakery.

"Shaun! How wonderful you look in your tailored coat." One lapel was lightly dusted with flour.

"I almost didn't recognize you," he boomed, nodding to Victoria, who swooped by, dancing the waltz. He nodded as if thanking her for pointing out the correct Autumn to him. Then he turned back to Autumn. "You look like a preacher's wife."

In the comfort of Shaun's firm embrace, she left for the dance floor and the new waltz that was beginning. Shaun was by far the best dancer she'd ever known, although she'd only known him for little more than a week.

She was determined to enjoy this evening. Tonight's social was a celebration of spring thaw, when the rivers opened up, when steamships arrived in the harbor after a long bleak winter, unloading hundreds of daring men and a few daring women in hopes of striking gold. Many were content to stay put in Skagway, to acclimatize to the weather and backwoods living, before facing the strenuous climb over the mountains to the Canadian Klondike.

They'd only completed one pleasant round of the waltz when Shaun was tapped on the shoulder.

That man again.

"A moment with your partner," the stranger asked, so much taller and darker than her blond baker. At the responding silence, the man's voice deepened. "For a wounded soldier who's returned from battle."

What battle? There was no battle she was aware of. Was he fibbing?

It worked on Shaun. He gave her up without a struggle. With annoyance, Autumn clamped her lips together.

"I'll be back with two drinks," said Shaun. "I'm parched. The ovens were hot tonight."

"But why—"

Shaun left.

With a slight smile of victory, the stranger cupped her right hand, and with his other hand on her waist, yanked her firmly to his chest. She sprang to life. Didn't he know the proper way to hold a woman? She wiggled her way out a bit and was grateful, for the first time this evening, that every inch of her body was clothed. It didn't stop him from glancing over the lace that ruffled her bosom. Her cheeks flamed.

Because there were so few women in Alaska, the town was filled with attention-starved men.

She strained a smile. "What battle do you come from? Somewhere overseas?"

"No battle. I only said that to get *him* out of the way."

Scoundrel. Her chin slackened with distaste.

"Oh, I do have scruples," he said, much to her displeasure that he could read her expression so accurately. "That's what got me into this mess. Justice and injustice."

What did he mean?

"Come."

Just like that. A command. He locked his fingers around her wrist and marched her toward the balcony. Insulted by the intimate gesture, she yanked free of his hot fingers.

Nevertheless, she saw Shaun headed that way, too, with two glasses of punch, so she reluctantly followed.

"You can remove your mask," the stranger said.

"As can you."

"I'm not wearing—" He dark eyes flicked, then he found humor in her words. "I told you. My name's irrelevant."

Never mind him. Where was Shaun? As they entered the cool outdoors, she swatted at the blackflies.

The outdoor balcony was surrounded by icy peaks. The midnight sun of Alaska blazed low between the shoulders of the mountains, casting a warm glow on all it touched. Twenty-four-hour sunlight. It was still a marvel to Autumn. She spotted the half-moon, high in the sky and tinged in blue, determined to shed some light on their balcony, too, even though outpowered by the sun a billion to one.

A handful of men stood near the stone ledge rail. Three dressed in miner's clothes immediately left, mumbling something about fresh drinks without the pesky flies, till there were only two remaining in the shadows. They were dressed more like ranchers than gentlemen at a dance.

Down below, on the path leading to the front door of the grand hotel, more folks were making their way through the heavy cedars.

Something dawned on her. Was this man an investor? Had the banker sent him? Smiling timidly, she stared at the turn of his dark cheek. Sunlight glinted off the clean lines of his jaw. His muscles strained against his jacket as he stepped back two paces. His face remained in shadow, almost as though he were trying to hide.

Attempting to figure things out, she looked past his heavy shoulders to the opened balcony door. There was poor Victoria, being dragged toward the stage.

"Oh, no," said Autumn beneath her breath. "They want her to sing."

"Pardon?" The stranger cocked his dark head.

"I need to go rescue someone."

"But I have something to ask you."

He *was* an investor. She could feel it. Something unspoken between them, a surge of magnetic excitement.

"You are Victoria Windhaven?"

She blinked at him. He had her wrong identity. Not an investor, after all.

Now she was getting angry. If he refused to give his name, why should she give hers? Shaun would soon set him straight. She took another step to get away, but he blocked her path.

"Do you travel with your medicine bag?" he asked.

"Of course not. This is a social event."

"Then you left it at the boardinghouse."

"Inside the front door. Left closet." That much she knew. But she was showing off, stretching this game too far. He would soon discover she had the upper hand here.

"It's a pity we're short of doctors," he said. "They tell me the last two headed for the Klondike a month ago."

"I…I understand a group of medical students will be arriving for the summer."

She wheeled around to his other side, but he simply leaned back against the stone wall and she was trapped again.

"What happened to the two other nurses who work for the Society?"

So he wasn't such a stranger. He knew the goings-on. Autumn glanced into the ballroom. Victoria was arguing with the two men leading her up the stage. At this rate, though, surely Victoria would win the fifty-dollar prize for best costume. "Left on a boat up the coast three days ago. A mountain fever has gripped Cedar Point. They're not sure if it's dysentery or cholera or something else. Two men have come down with it."

The planes of his face twisted. "That's a shame."

She didn't like how close he was standing, mere inches away. She stared at the white patches on his skin. "You normally have a beard. Your face is lighter where the sun hasn't hit."

He angled his head away from her, but she noticed something else. Fading light caught the tiny hair clippings at his ear.

"You just got your hair cut."

Why would someone get their hair cut the very minute before a dance? Had he been in that much of a rush?

Behind him on the stage, Victoria was raising her hand to her face, about to unmask.

But here in front of Autumn, oblivious to the stage, the stranger's riveting gaze made her tense. There was something contrary in his eyes. A black glint of trouble.

An icy fever raced up the back of her neck.

Sensing danger, she stumbled backward across her petticoat and long suede skirt. She leaped to run, but it was too late. He called to the two men hidden in shadow, and as silent as an ocean wave in moonlight, one clamped a hand over her mouth and they slid her over the balcony to two more outstretched hands waiting in the shrubs.

Her heart thrust against her ribs. She kicked and bit and swung her arms into jaws and chests.

"Leave me alone," she shouted between the trees. "They'll kill you! My friends will kill you!"

They shoved a kerchief across her mouth. Her heart roared against the whipping Alaskan wind.

What did he want from her? *Who was this criminal?*

Chapter Two

The thing she didn't understand, thought Quinn Rowlan, biting down on his indignation in their canoe, was that he'd do anything to save his brother. Two hours later and she was still fighting. Quinn wasn't proud of the abduction, but he knew the young nurse would never come willingly. Especially if she knew who *he* was. His muscles tensed with the outrage of being so wrongly accused by people who didn't know him.

"Stop moving," he commanded her.

She was seated and struggling between him and his friend Jackson. Jackson Langford was so tall and skinny, it was hard for him to balance in the canoe.

Behind them in a second birch-bark canoe, Ben Wilks and Trevor McCabe were keeping up.

"We'll tip," Quinn warned her, "you'll freeze in the water and we'll still haul you with us. I won't hurt you, I promise. But don't hurt yourself."

With her mouth gagged by a white handkerchief, her hands loosely bound behind her, she stopped kicking and the canoe calmed.

Quinn stopped paddling from the back end of the canoe in order to lean toward her.

She flinched, but he was only reaching for her mask. With a tug, he slid it down around her throat. Her hair was another matter. The rich chestnut-brown strands, so neatly pinned in place at the masquerade ball, were coming undone.

"There now. Shame to cover those lovely eyes."

Her wide brown eyes cut right through him.

Guilt stung his cheeks again. Ignoring the feeling, he picked up his oar and continued with his strokes.

He had changed back into his denims and Stetson, disposing of the suit he'd bought in haste from the unknown barber in town, but she was still in fancy skirts. The long leather duster he'd supplied to protect her from the frigid air covered most of her. However, her long legs slid out from beneath the tan leather, revealing the thick leather belt that circled her tiny waist, and the billowing blouse that rose over her chest. The red suede skirt was already getting stained with water.

Wispy strands of dark hair fell across her neck and down her shoulders, gathering at the see-through lace that barely stretched across her bosom. If she'd aimed to conceal her body in that blouse, its conservative nature only accentuated the curves beneath, making her an intriguing blend of churchlike propriety mixed with smoldering sex.

Her cheeks glimmered in the twilight; her lips bit into the rag.

"Untie her mouth," Quinn ordered Jackson, keeping still in the tight space of the canoe. "She can scream all she wants in this wilderness. No one can hear."

"You sure, Quinn?" Jackson hesitated to move closer.

Her eyes blinked at the call of his name.

"Yeah."

When Jackson untied the gag, she spit out the rag and turned her horrified gaze to Quinn. "What do you want?"

Shame sprang through him, but his brother desperately needed her and there was no time to coax her gently.

"Your help."

She huffed in disgust. The sound echoed over the water, past the two men coming up in the canoe beside them. "There are kinder methods of asking."

Her voice was tough, but her knees trembled beneath the red suede. She gazed at the guns on Quinn's hips, then she searched the other men for their weapons. He groaned. If her intent was to fight them, her slender build was no match for any of his muscled men. She looked to the second canoe and when she spotted her medicine bag, she jarred. Two hours earlier, he'd informed his men where she kept it, and they'd quickly retrieved it.

"I apologize for the force. But if I had asked you

nicely to come with me for a few days, would you have said yes?"

She lifted her chin. *"A few days?"*

"We both know what your answer would've been."

She sank onto the hard wooden plank of her seat. Dim light streaming from the thick forest captured the turn of her cheek and the straight bridge of her nose. The scent of grasses and wildflowers drenched the moist air.

Sitting still, she stared at her medicine bag as though trying to fathom what was happening. Wasn't it obvious? Most folks came gently to ask for aid, Quinn imagined. They likely paid her with gifts of food and personal items difficult to buy here in Alaska, and how had he come? With guns and ropes.

But his brother was near death. And due to circumstances beyond Quinn's control, no one in town would risk their own safety to help his gang.

This nurse would tend to the festering stab wound, would provide medicine to get rid of the fever. Quinn would then apologize profusely, pay her fifty times her usual amount and secretly return her home.

Simple.

If only she'd stop looking at him as though he were a monster.

I'm not Victoria, Autumn wanted to scream, moments after they removed the cloth from her mouth. Should she?

Trying to appear calm in the canoe although her

heart was ripping like thunder, she weighed her options. She was outnumbered four to one. Her hands were tied, so there was little she could accomplish by jumping overboard. She couldn't grab for any guns. Shouting for help would do little on this desolate river.

She stared over the shoulder of the red-haired one they called Jackson and ignored the leader, Quinn, seated behind her, even though she felt *his* stare on her shoulders, her face.

They believed she was Victoria. They believed she had skills in medicine. Obviously, this man had shaved and carefully dressed in preparation for the masquerade ball, concealing his true identity. Even if she were the best nurse in the world, how could she nurture cold-blooded criminals?

Why else would they be hiding their identities? They were killers and thieves.

And what of her identity?

When they discovered she wasn't who they thought, what would they do to her? Take a knife to her innards and toss her to the bottom of the glacial riverbed?

She shook with fear.

Then, unable to bear the circumstance, she buried her face in the damp leather lapel of her borrowed duster. It smelled of *him*. Faint shaving tonics. She turned away from the scent, preferring to hold her face to the biting wind.

If she spoke up and told them she wasn't Victoria, would they kill her and return for the real one? Then her friend would be in danger.

But they were a good ways from Skagway now. Wouldn't Victoria be safely protected? This gang wouldn't dare go back.

Everyone in town would be searching for Autumn. Victoria would be alarmed at her sudden disappearance. She'd notify all their friends—Shaun and Gilbert and even Cornelius. They'd tell the deputy marshal and he'd form a posse. In fact, Deputy Marshal Brander had *been* there, as a witness. The lawman was astute and saw things most folks didn't. He was doing something right now. He was searching. He was.

Maybe these brutal men would let her go when they realized they'd made a horrible mistake. Would they desert her in the wilderness? Would they kill her because she was a witness to something she didn't even realize?

They had *kidnapped* her, which added to their list of crimes.

She murmured another prayer.

The canoes quickly sped past a bend in the river, to her surprise, the men docked at a grassy slope. Two other empty canoes sat perched along the sandy riverbank, plus a small rowboat. Beyond the clump of skinny pines—the spruce and hemlock trees—six horses grazed beside a log cabin. Judging by the smoke puffing from the chimney, someone was inside.

Her heart sped. Her eyes widened. Frantic, she scurried to sit up to protect herself from a beating, or whatever else was coming, but Jackson disembarked alone. This allowed the leader, Quinn, to help her out of the canoe.

"Is it safe to untie your hands?" he asked.

"Yes…."

His jaw hardened. "This isn't the normal way I go about doing things. I promise to let you go as soon as…as soon as you help my brother."

Brother. So that's who needed her help.

She shuddered. Her legs wobbled.

"Come with me," Quinn ordered her. "I want you to work quickly."

Quinn hauled her by the elbow. Then with a snap of the cloth binding her wrists, he freed her.

She rubbed the sore spots and kept her eyes on Quinn's guns as he pulled the medical bag from the canoe. She'd only fired once in her life, at a quail her grandfather had tried to show her how to hunt. She'd missed, more out of fear for wounding the wildfowl than anything else. It had been difficult enough aiming for a bird. How could she aim at a person?

Easy. It was them or her.

This was her moment. She'd tell him he'd made an unbelievable error in judgment and…and if he were true to his word…

As his fingers wrapped around the medicine bag, she blurted, "I'm not Victoria Windhaven."

The leather bag swung against his thigh. He straightened up beside her on the angled riverbank, wind curling at his Stetson, darkness glinting from his eyes.

"Two people pointed you out."

"It was a masquerade."

His stare was cold and hard. "Two people."

"I was standing beside the real Victoria. They were…they were pointing at her."

"I called you by name and you didn't deny it."

"It was an act. I'm not a nurse. I…I work in the hotel."

Moments passed. They seemed the longest in the world. His expression remained unmoved.

"Nice try." He grasped her elbow and dragged her toward the cabin.

"I'm not Victoria!"

"If you attempt any tricks to harm my brother…if this is your way of confusing things…"

"It's not, it's not. I'm wearing a wig. I don't know anything about medicine!"

He dragged her inside the log hut. She could smell the sickness before she saw it. Nausea rushed up her throat. She'd always had a weak stomach.

Quinn nudged her past the burning logs in the fireplace but she couldn't look at the man lying in the cot against the wall.

Quinn asked her in a kinder tone, "I'd be much obliged if you could help my brother, Harrison. He was stabbed three days ago. He's burning with a fever."

The wounded man moaned. Autumn's sentiments stirred. Quinn tossed the bag to the foot of the bed, then grabbed her shoulders so she was forced to look at his brother.

Stabbed. Who had they tried to rob? Or kill?

He was younger than Quinn, but dark haired, too. And afraid. His eyes were watery and he was shaking harder than she was. Sweat drenched his bare chest. Someone had packed gauze linen into his bleeding ribs. Fresh blood soaked the area. Lots of blood, covering everything.

It was impossible to hold down her stomach. Bile pushed up her throat. She lunged for the door. Quinn tried to hold her back, maybe thinking she was trying to bolt, but she begged free and thankfully made it down the front stoop and into the shrubs, where she retched.

"Do you think she's got that mountain fever? Maybe she came in contact with those other nurses who were tryin' to help." Jackson was almost done packing the horses as he spoke to Quinn.

"Could be," Quinn answered, packing his own mare. He'd deduced her sickness from the minute he'd seen her vomit.

It was close to midnight and Quinn's eyes strained with exhaustion. He and his men had been up for nearly forty-eight hours. Ben and Trevor were inside, rousing Harrison. Quinn's fifth man, Vic Nixon, was feeding the horses.

Quinn didn't for a moment believe she wasn't the nurse. If he were in her position, wouldn't he try the same ploy?

"I had cholera once." Jackson hoisted his saddlebags to the horse. "Made me puke every time I stood up. Had the runs, too. I had to sleep near the can all night. It spreads easy."

And it's deadly, thought Quinn.

Exasperated, he pushed back his Stetson and shoved his brother's few clothes into another saddle-bag. He stared at the young woman seated on the log pile ten feet away from everyone else, shivering beneath the long leather coat.

"Isn't this great? I brought back a sick woman," said Quinn. "Whatever she's got, if she gave it to Harrison, it could kill him if the wound doesn't."

"We gotta leave her behind."

Quinn sighed. "I'm damned no matter what I do. If I leave her and she gets real sick, she can't fend on her own. She might die. If I take her, the rest of us might get it."

"Leave her behind," Jackson repeated. But he wouldn't meet Quinn's gaze as he tied a frying pan to his horse's pack. "It's best for her. There'll be more folks travelin' along the river. They'll stop and help. Maybe even that posse she's probably hopin' for."

How could Quinn desert her? She was here because he *took* her.

"Miss?" he hollered.

She looked up from her hanky, eyes swollen and cheeks pale.

"Do you have any medicine in that bag of yours that might help you?"

"*Me?*"

"With the mountain fever."

She didn't seem to understand what he was saying. Her posture wilted. She sank her face into her hands. Was she that ill already?

"Oh," she said. "Right." The thought seemed to oddly cheer her. She perked up on the logs. "No, I'm afraid there isn't any potion to alleviate the sickness. You best all stay away from me. Three men at Cedar Point have already died from it."

"Three? I thought you said two. And you never mentioned anyone dying."

"Well…two initially. But then three. Likely more by now. And I didn't want to mention how gravely ill they were at the ball. I mean, it was a social event."

Hell.

They were running out of time and he had to figure out what to do. He'd check on Harrison, and then talk about how to bring her along. He'd be the one to share a horse with her. Someone had to, and she *was* his responsibility, wasn't she?

Stepping into the cabin, Quinn nodded to Ben and Trevor, who were getting Harrison to his feet. Earlier, Quinn had given him a shot of whiskey, trying to drown his brother's moans of agony.

"Go pack your horses," Quinn told them. "I'll get him to his feet."

They obeyed and Quinn struggled to lift his brother. Shaky boots hit the floor.

"How am I…supposed to ride a horse?"

"We got a small sled hitched to one of 'em. I

figure we'll head to the fishing village. Kirkland. We might flag down an incoming ship. Possible doctors on board. They'll help us if we get to them before they reach Skagway and see our faces on those Wanted posters."

Along the way, he would drop off the woman somewhere close to home. He wasn't planning on telling her any of this. If she had a hint of where they were headed, she'd likely pass it on to the law. Quinn was sorry he'd ever attempted to gain her help, and sorry for what he'd put her through.

But he'd done what he had to, and now it was time to let her go. She was a nurse, she'd tell approaching people who she was and warn them not to get too close. When she made it home, it would be easier to isolate herself and her sickness in a room somewhere than on the road with them.

They shuffled out to the porch and Harrison nearly collapsed. "Let me just—" he wheezed "—sit here a minute."

Quinn let him be. He surveyed the site. Almost cleared up. His men were at the horses.

Where was the nurse?

His pulse kicked up a notch. He grabbed at the brim of his Stetson and peered through the scraggy pines.

Where was she?

He leaped off the porch and looked to his right. Then his left. His gut churned with a dozen possibilities.

In mounting apprehension, he strode through the camp. "Anyone see the woman?"

"No," they hollered. Jackson dropped his reins and the others rushed to help.

Quinn saw her first. Her leather duster flashed at him through the woods, somewhere along the river. A flicker of tan. Panting, he ran through the trees to the shoreline. She was already ten feet away in the rowboat. Frantic at seeing him, she raced away in the current.

"Come back here," he ordered.

Her face buckled with determination. She pushed harder on the oars.

"You don't know what you're up against," he shouted. "The rivers are teeming with dangerous men!"

"You!"

"I'm not an outlaw!"

She pounded the oars through the water, getting better at the strokes. "Right! Only decent men steal women!"

"That's not... Come back here!"

She rowed faster, almost around the bend now. Desperate, he waded into the river, boots and all.

She yelped, "Get away from me!"

Jackson was behind her on the riverbank, but she couldn't see him. Quinn signaled for him to climb into the water behind her boat. At the same time, Quinn rushed right at her through the frigid water as it rose toward his crotch. He reached for his holster to lift his guns and keep them dry, but she must've thought he was reaching for his weapons.

He didn't know *she* had a gun.

She raised her revolver, cocked the hammer and

then with a heavy sigh, lowered the gun as if she couldn't pull the trigger after all. With relief, he barreled toward her.

Just as Jackson reached her from behind and swooped down toward her shoulder, she lifted the gun again. And blasted.

Chapter Three

Autumn hadn't meant to shoot.

The power of the explosion ripped up her shoulder and knocked her off her feet. She landed on her backside in the rowboat as it spun around from Quinn. The shot was a mistake. She was lowering the gun for the second time, but something had bumped the boat from behind and her fear had caused her to jump.

A mighty hand came down upon her shoulder. She jumped from fright. It was Jackson, hovering above her. *He* had shoved the boat, likely to ruin her aim, but had instead scared her.

He snatched the fallen gun from the steel hull. "If you killed him…you better pray for your soul, lady."

His words ignited terror within her. She pushed up against Jackson's grip, stuck her head out of the boat and peered at what she'd done.

Quinn had plunged into the water. His men came running.

Lord, she'd shot another person. "I'm sorry," she murmured.

But then Quinn rose and sputtered in her direction.

"Holy hell," said Jackson.

Riveted on Quinn, she couldn't breathe. He was unharmed. She sank onto her seat. He cursed and got his bearings, all the while his heated brown eyes targeting her.

She'd missed.

She pulled her shoulders higher and controlled her strained breathing. "You tried to shoot me. You tried to shoot me *first*."

"I was lifting my guns to keep them out of the water." His tone was menacing as he stood there, drenched.

"You didn't do a…a very good job."

An icy quiet took hold of the gang as they stared from this man, Quinn, to her. He was shaking his head, visibly trying to contain his outrage at what she'd just attempted.

"It was a mistake. I didn't mean to shoot."

His voice was a threatening rumble. "But you did."

What would they do to her? Her eardrums throbbed in time with her pulse.

Jackson gave her boat another unexpected shove and she lunged toward the shoreline and four angry men. In the distance at the cabin, Harrison had slumped to one side on the porch.

"Need help gettin' out, Quinn?" his men asked.

"No." He dragged himself out of the chilly water to a dry piece of grass. Someone tossed him his wet hat. He fingered the brim and set his sights on her. He was a menacing brute with sharp black eyes and dark shadow covering his cheeks.

With a swagger, he strode to Jackson, took the gun out of his hand, examined the grip and held it in the air, as if coming to some sort of conclusion.

"Vic!" yelled Quinn.

Cringing, the young man with the baby face stepped forward and took it. "Sorry. I set it down beside my horse."

Autumn watched for signs of movement toward her, but quickly realized no one was coming after her. Likely, they still assumed she had mountain fever. She had tried to tell Quinn the truth, that she wasn't a nurse, but he hadn't accepted it. Too stubborn to let himself admit *he* could make such a blunder.

The cool night wind whipped across her face. If she let them all believe she was indeed Victoria, she would remain protected. Isolated. They definitely didn't want her going anywhere near the injured brother, in case her illness caused his death. How odd that this tangle of lies was now working to her benefit.

She rose to her booted feet and disembarked from the boat. Her heavy suede skirt dragged along the mud. She snatched at her hems. Jackson and one of the younger men backed away from her. She had that much power? It invigorated her.

She turned to Quinn.

He was catching his breath, a huge hulk of muscle

standing in the dim cast of the moon and the eerie twilight of the midnight sun.

"I think you should leave me behind," she said, gaining courage. "You should leave me right here on this riverbank."

Quinn stared at the stubborn woman. He felt his muscles stiffen in the frigid air. He needed to get out of his wet clothes, and fast.

"You don't look sick," he said. "You look tired, but not sick."

She coughed and clutched her side.

"You'll ride with me," he finally said after trying to decide whether she was being truthful or not. "We've been in close contact already."

"But I'm ill. Leave me here."

"Get me some dry clothes," Quinn snapped at his men, ignoring her request.

Twenty-one-year-old Vic ran toward the horses. "Got it!"

Quinn unbuttoned his shirt, revealing a bare chest.

With an embarrassed cough, she looked away. He kept going. She'd just tried to *kill* him. To hell with courtesies, he thought.

"Despite what you think of me, I won't leave you here alone." He ripped off his shirt and toweled off with a clean rag Jackson tossed. "You'll get yourself together and you'll follow my orders. Understand?"

She slowly nodded. He still planned to release her,

to get this troublemaker off his hands, and she'd just proved he couldn't trust her with any information.

"One more thing," he said, jabbing the towel at his chest. "If you ever, *ever,* take aim at me again—" He choked on the words. "Your life was *never* in danger. Do you hear me!"

She lowered her head. Her long dark hair tangled at her shoulders. Her duster opened to reveal a starched lace collar that had lost its bounce.

And suddenly, he was sick of it all. Sick of fighting on the side of right, when everyone saw him on the side of wrong. Sick of trying to prove himself against a system of corrupted law. Mostly, he was sick of not being able to connect with women of his choosing. Women like this one, proper and decent. Like her, he wanted all the good things in life, but in the last two years, he always—*always*—got nothing but agony and sorrow for his troubles.

Why the hell bother with any of it anymore?

So his name would never be cleared. Who the hell cared, and what did he matter to anyone?

Autumn watched Quinn as she wiped mud off her boots. Quinn was attentive to his brother. The rest of the men were packing around her, mindful to keep themselves yards away from her, but her eyes strayed to the dark man in the black shirt and fringed, tan suede jacket. Quinn eased Harrison onto a handmade deerskin sling that was strapped to the back of Jackson's horse. Quinn's face skewered with sympathy every time his little brother winced.

She supposed even criminals cared deeply for their family. She, too, couldn't help but be touched by the young man's plight. Her lips moved softly as she murmured at his pain.

At least Harrison's harsh breathing had become more even. His chest was rising equally on both sides, despite the wounded ribs. His nostrils were no longer flaring, as if begging for oxygen, and the tugging at the hollow of his throat had left. Still, he had the fever, shivering one minute, throwing off his fox furs the next. He was a stranger to her, the reason she was here, yet she supposed he had nothing to do with his brother's plan to abduct a nurse.

Who were these men and what were they running from?

Quinn turned to Autumn, ten yards away. He surprised her with his next question. "What can I give him for the pain?"

Her lashes fluttered as she considered the question. When her grandpa was dying, the doctor had ordered lots of laudanum.

Quinn yanked open her medical bag and peered in. Obviously, neither he nor she could administer a needle of morphine.

"There must be laudanum in there that he could drink," she hollered.

Quinn found a brown bottle, poured the liquid

opiate and alcohol mixture into a tin cup and gave it to his brother. Harrison sputtered as he drank.

From her far left, tall and skinny Jackson tossed her a strip of smoked venison. "Better eat while you can."

She was starving, and bit in. A hunk of bread came next, followed by her own canteen filled with water.

Twenty minutes later, she was standing beside Quinn and his mare. The coat of his spotted Appaloosa shimmered with health.

By the sun, it was two or three in the morning already. Lord, she was tired. Her lids were so dry they squeaked. She hadn't dared to remove her wig. She'd mentioned it to him earlier, but wished she hadn't. She needed him to believe she was a nurse who required quarantine. Besides, the wig was keeping her head warm, and protecting her scalp from the gnawing blackflies.

"The laudanum worked," he said, peering over at his sleeping brother. "Thanks."

She gulped. "Right." And then she couldn't stop herself from offering more advice. "My grandfather once had a cyst removed. Later…there was an abscess. To drain the wound, they had to put a gauze wick in it. The pus came up through the cotton. Someone might have to do that for your brother."

"Someone?"

She shifted beneath his stare. "If I go near his wound, I might contaminate it."

"Right," he said, staring at her. "Germs."

She looked away and pretended she hadn't said anything.

Quinn spread a gray wool blanket beneath his saddle. It was big enough to hang over the horse's hindquarters, which left enough room for her to sit. She was thankful she wouldn't have to ride completely bareback.

The other four men on horseback rode out. Jackson hauled Harrison behind him, while young Vic had tied Harrison's golden palomino behind his own.

High in his saddle, Quinn extended his hand to Autumn. "Have you ridden much?"

"Haven't been on a horse since I was fourteen." Truth was, she found horses to be terribly large and intimidating.

Quinn had no outward reaction. "Where you from?"

"Seattle."

"Ah, that explains it."

Facing the inevitable—*him*—she grasped his hand. He gripped tight and she swung up hard behind him. "What do you mean?"

"With all the rain you get, you people are apparently better with umbrellas than horses."

She ignored his attempt at humor. Then thought better of it and forced an insincere smile. First chance she got, she would slip off this horse and run for freedom. In all the chaos, she'd almost forgotten about her appointment with the credit manager Monday afternoon. Yes, yes, if she focused on her normal routine, she could keep her mind clear.

Monday, her loan would be approved. Tuesday, she'd be the proud new owner of the Imperial Hotel.

But the overwhelming fear of possibly never escaping gripped her. Desperate to play her game of survival, she hung loosely to the side of his jacket, pretending to cooperate.

The horse's moving muscles beneath her thighs felt strange. She had to dig her knees into horseflesh to get her balance. It didn't help that Quinn's huge shoulders were right in front of her face. His power made her jittery.

His guns, wrapped around his hips, were only a foot away from her eager fingers. She needed to lull him into trusting her. "My grandpa used to ride his horse while holding his umbrella. There's quite an art to it."

Quinn turned his dark face toward her. "That so? How did *you* get around?"

"Umbrella and mule."

His shoulders twitched. "That was more your speed, I suppose."

"Martha was dependable. Much more dependable than any man I ever met in Seattle."

Was that a low thread of laughter coming from his throat? He seemed almost human.

"Hold tighter."

For her own good, she would follow his orders. She pressed in closer to his jacket and wrapped herself as tightly around him as she could. His hard, firm muscles flexed beneath her fingers.

The gang entered the damp woods. There were

patches of cold brown earth in the hollows where nothing was flowering yet, despite it being early June. In other sunnier spots, crocuses were in full purple bloom. It didn't take her long to get the hang of riding. It wasn't much different from Martha. Except Autumn was sitting much higher up on this horse, and didn't control the reins. In fact, she controlled nothing at all.

They talked no more for over an hour. And as hard as she stretched, she could not reach his guns.

At this proximity, though, she noticed a lot about him. He had a firm jaw, bristly cheeks and straight black eyebrows that offset his thick wavy hair. He was a handsome enough man. Overall, in fine physical form. Excellent form. Why did he lead such a criminal life? There was plenty of work in Alaska for men who wanted it, a big town to live in, a few available women who'd gladly take in a healthy man who looked like he could outwork several. Didn't he want a wife? Children who could look up to him?

She pitied him.

They trudged on through changing landscape. The riverbanks turned into wide, sandy dunes that stretched for an acre before meeting up with ribbons of forest. The mountains had closed in, but they were basking in warm sunshine. Seabirds cawed in the blue sky, which she took to mean they were close to the ocean.

Quinn called out to Jackson to take the next bump with greater care, and groaned when the blackflies swarmed Harrison's face. At one point, Quinn hopped off his mare to cut a long branch with many leaves and used it to swat at the flies surrounding his sleeping brother.

"We'll make camp here," Quinn said, a while later.

Autumn's thighs seemed permanently stretched into a painful position. The muscles in her buttocks screeched with agony when she stumbled off the horse onto solid ground.

Thirty minutes later they had a fire going. Two. One for the other men, and one for her and Quinn, isolating her from the rest of the group.

Quinn raised his head, his Stetson firmly outlined between the shadows of the trees. "Shh," he told her as he scanned the forest.

She listened to the wind. Nothing unusual. Little birds chirping. The river flowing. Crackling from the campsite of the other men.

"It's nothing," he said.

She eased into the bedroll he'd provided. The cold blankets felt like an ice block against her limbs. She kicked her feet in the space to warm up. He watched her from across the fire in his own wool bedding.

This time, he kept his shirt on. She recalled the earlier vision when he'd stripped from his wet clothes. His chest was tanned by the sun, muscles that stretched from one broad shoulder to the other, accentuating his physique. His strength was intimidating, whether he wore a shirt or not.

His mouth revealed the most about him. The way he twitched his lips when he was concerned about his brother, or pressed them together when contemplating her.

"One of two things is going to happen when I shut my eyes," he said. "One, you'll try and run. You could get pretty far. At least to the river. Maybe even straight to the ocean. But there are six sets of ears waiting to hear you do it."

"I thought you were going to set me free."

"Not till I know it's safe for all of us."

She ached to believe him.

"What's the other thing?"

"You'll shut your eyes, too."

"Hmm." She did yearn for sleep. She was drugged with fatigue. Wouldn't it be better to make a run for it when they got to the ocean's edge? At least then she'd know which direction to run— anywhere up and down the coast toward people, ships or Skagway.

It was early Sunday morning. She had a day and a half to get to her appointment. *Please.* Heaven help this man if he stood in her way. Monday was her last chance for victory, her last appointment with one of the few bankers who had agreed to see her.

Slyly, she adjusted her wig, which had slipped an inch backward. When she looked up, his head was cocked to the wind again.

"What do you hear?" she whispered, getting frightened.

"Something in the river." He looked to his men. They were gearing down for sleep. Quinn raised his arm in some sort of signal. Jackson listened for a minute, then signaled back. All clear.

Even so, Quinn drew his gun, jumped to his feet and walked around. Whatever it was, five minutes later he dismissed it. When he came back to the fire, he planted his holster close to his bedroll. He was scaring her.

"What in tarnation is out there?" she asked.

"Wild animals." He left his boots on while attempting sleep. She did the same. In case she got an opportunity to run.

"You said you had a grandpa. Any other family?"

She looked to the sizzling logs. "All gone."

"Your folks?"

Was it necessary to talk? If she didn't answer, would it upset him? "Died of smallpox when I was six months old."

"So…no brothers or sisters, either."

"No."

A big family was something she longed for. A husband, children. She'd never take them for granted. She wasn't old enough when her parents had passed to even recall what they looked like, and they'd been too poor for photographs. Elizabeth and William MacNeil. Strong names to be proud of.

Autumn stiffened as she stared at his dark face, telling herself never to trust him. There were a million things she wanted to ask him, too, but she was terrified of making him mad. He was just starting to relax around her. The more relaxed he became, the easier her escape.

"I've been thinking," he declared several minutes later, rising to poke the fire, "about what you said."

She hiked her shoulder up defensively as she wrapped her fingers into the blanket and scooped it under her chin. "What exactly?"

"That you're not Victoria Windhaven."

Her breath got tangled in her throat. The crackling of the logs seemed to shoot straight through her.

He *had* to believe she was Victoria. The situation had turned, and they *had* to go on believing she had the mountain sickness. If not, she'd be in physical danger from the rest of the men.

She sat up, the blanket wrapped around her waist, and tried to confuse him. "I was scared to admit it at first…. That I'm Victoria."

"You know when I finally realized you're not?"

Her heart bounced. She couldn't speak.

"When you suggested laudanum."

"It's common—"

"Yes, but the way you said it. You said 'There *must be* some in there.' You didn't say there *was* some in the bag, you said there must be, as if you didn't know."

She closed her eyes and flashed them open again in fear.

He was right here in front of her, on his knees beside the blessed warmth of the fire. He lifted his arm and before she realized what he intended, he slipped the wig off her head. Her natural blond hair, which she had pinned at the crown, slipped and anchored itself over one ear. A cold draft blew over her scalp.

His voice softened. "Now would be a good time to tell me your real name."

"Oh," she murmured.

Breathless, he waited for an answer.

Her heart drummed with fear as her mind swirled with possible responses. Should she lie? Should she tell him the truth? This brute was capable of anything.

Chapter Four

"Answer me first," she finally said, defiantly raising her shoulders as she sat on the firm ground in front of him. Quinn watched the firelight swirl over her cheeks. Moonlight trickled down between the trees. The sky was an odd purple, still infused with the sun. The great orange ball was only several degrees below the horizon, not enough to block the effect of its rays. It felt peculiar, so far from North Dakota, to be lit by fire, moon and sun, all at the same time. Almost as disorienting as staring at this beautiful stranger.

She pulled her knees to her chest, as if forming a shield between her body and his, and asked directly, "How did your brother get stabbed?"

Quinn winced. How much could he tell her? She'd surely use it against them at her first opportunity. Hell, she'd fired a gun straight at him, so she wasn't afraid to fight back.

The worst thing was… The worst thing was, he

thought as he kneeled before her, fire heating his backside…he would've fired the gun, too.

He watched her ball of blond hair collapse under the strain of pins and fall to her shoulder. Blond suited her better than brunette—the gold glimmers softened her sharp cheekbones and gushed color into her fair skin. He tossed her wig onto her blanket.

"Harrison's story," he said, "is not for sensitive ears."

The brown flecks in her eyes deepened. "Sensitive?" She grappled with the word. "When my grandpa died, I was forced to beg the landlord not to throw me and my grandmother out on the streets— he did so nonetheless. On the ship to Alaska, we lost three passengers to dysentery. I heard them vomiting all night in the cabin next to mine, yet couldn't do a thing to help them. Having been in Skagway for almost a year, I've seen two men gunned down in cold blood. Another blinded permanently by the snow. And I try to sympathize, not condemn, the house full of prostitutes three blocks away from the hotel. What, exactly, is so dainty about my life?"

He was riveted by this woman. Proper and feminine on the outside, but as tough as hooves on the inside.

"I'm sorry," he whispered. He reached out and drew a line at the base of her jaw with his finger. So soft. Like a silky milkweed. She remained still and silent, but he saw the tug at her throat, and it belied her calmness. "You're not the nurse. And I misbehaved badly."

"Misbehaved? You broke the law. And you're scaring the hell out of me."

Shame pricked his skin. His parents hadn't worked their backs to the breaking point on a dried-up ranch to raise him to treat a woman this way. Yet those same folks, his folks, looking down from heaven, would understand what he was trying to do for Harrison.

Quinn dropped his hand. "I'm truly sorry. And you don't have to be afraid, Miss…"

She searched his face, and perhaps what she saw was truth. "Autumn MacNeil."

"Autumn MacNeil," he repeated, liking the sound. "Miss Autumn MacNeil. That's very pretty. I've known an April and a May, but never an Autumn."

She didn't respond to his ribbing.

"You don't have the mountain fever, do you, Autumn?"

"I might have," she said gently, in the warm glow of the campfire. "If…if Victoria came in contact with it, then I might have it, as well."

"You don't."

She exhaled with a storm, as if knowing it, too.

Thank God, he thought. He hadn't put Harrison in further danger by thrusting a contagious woman at him.

But what of her? He noted the fear that caused her lip to tremble, and thus leaned back on his haunches. "You felt safer letting us believe it."

"So?"

He rumbled a breath of exclamation, barely audible. Yeah, so?

He moved back to his side of the fire. She drew her blankets up to her chin and waited for his response.

He pointed in the direction of his men. "So…I'll let them go on believing it."

Her oval eyes widened. "You're not going to tell them?"

"It's the least I can do to make you feel safer." He knew his men would never cross the line with this young miss. Never in a hundred years would they do her harm. But she didn't know it, and it became extremely important to him, for some inexplicable reason, to make her *feel* it.

Five minutes later, Autumn was still watching Quinn. She guarded her breath, trying to be patient. After he had exchanged signals with the man guarding the other camp, and was satisfied that his wounded brother was comfortable and sleeping, Quinn slid into his bedroll. The wool blanket wasn't nearly long enough to cover him, she noted. He kept his clothes on.

Was he going to release her? Was he going to say "You're welcome to leave anytime you want"?

"Vic's staying up all night, in case you're wondering. He's got my orders to tie you up if you try anything."

With a groan of defiance, Autumn rolled onto her makeshift pillow—her borrowed leather duster turned inside out to its linen lining. Everything he'd told her was a heap of manure.

Now he expected her to close her eyes? Close her

eyes in the midst of all these men, and trust them not to come near her?

With the pretense of doing so, she turned to face him and stubbornly kept her eyes wide open.

He could barely hold himself alert. His lids fluttered toward the fire, over her body, then back up to her face. With another flick, he closed them. Moments went by and she realized he must be dog-tired after missing sleep for forty-eight hours. She'd heard the men talking earlier, and since Vic had stayed behind to watch Harrison while the other four had traveled by canoe to bring her back, Vic had been the only one to catch any sleep in two days.

Her spirits lifted. Quinn would soon be in a deep slumber. Was this her chance? Why wait for him to make the decision of when and where to release her?

If at all.

With her heart tripling in speed, she kept her head still on the leather coat but shifted her gaze to the other site.

The young man, Vic, was engrossed in watching the flames of his fire. He tilted his short legs toward the heat and removed his hat, which made his smooth cheeks look as plump as two turnips. All six horses were tied ten yards behind him, obstructed from her view by a string of cedars. He turned a quick look in her direction and she held her breath, eyes open. She needn't worry, she reminded herself, for half her body was hidden by brush, twelve inches high. Vic turned back to his fire.

He couldn't possibly see much of her, unless she rose and walked around. She lifted her head and saw the other four men dozing, with Harrison having been lifted from his sling to a spot close to their fire.

A log beyond her boots popped in the flames. Quinn startled out of his sleep, flashed his eyes open at the flames, then at her, at the same time reaching for his holster. She closed her eyes, feigning sleep, and through several pulse-escalating moments, she waited.

Nothing.

Opening them slowly again, she was relieved to see his eyes closed. His forehead was creased, even in his sleep, as though still worried about his brother, or perhaps the other troubles that plagued him. The firm jaw that'd been so carefully shaved for the masquerade ball was shadowed by new growth. The harsh line of his lips had softened in the blaze of the fire. At least something was easier about him. Certainly not his muscled frame in his black cotton shirt, and the sheer overwhelming size of his shoulders. His heavy breathing mixed with the sounds of the fire—jittery pops of dried bark—and the howling sizzle of wet timber as water oozing from its rings was instantly boiled. Even the wind sounded lonesome as it shushed through the leaves around them.

One of his guns was visible. The one on his left side where the blanket was pulled away.

She waited for what she guessed to be twenty minutes, perhaps thirty, before she stirred again. Ever so slowly, she rose to her knees. Crouching behind the shrubs between her fire and the other, she clutched her rolled-up duster and inched past Quinn. She stopped at his hips.

With shaky nerves, knowing how much depended on this moment, Autumn pressed her fingers to the crisscrossed hatching of his gun's walnut grip, waited for the fire to crack again to hide any noise she might make, then quickly and smoothly withdrew.

Lord, it was heavy. Six chambers glittered in slivers of moonlight. Metal and wood. Shiny and attractive in a murderous sort of way.

It took her another fifteen minutes to crawl slowly from the fire to the edge of the forest. She warned herself to go slow, no matter how tempted she was to flee.

Once she got past the edge of the clearing to the thicker part of the forest, she rose to full height and ripped full force through the trees.

It was about ten minutes later, maybe twenty, when she heard the faint whistle.

They knew!

Digging deep to a reserve she wasn't sure she had, she lifted her legs higher, ran faster, sucked for more air when her sides were already bursting with pain. She ignored the leaves thrashing against her cheeks, and held that gun with muscles nearly tearing out of her shoulder.

When she reached the river, beyond the forest in an open clearing between the mountains, the darkness lifted. The mix of moon and sun lit the trees and grasses clear enough that she could see every reed she was crunching through.

Two of the whistles faded, became almost silent. One was getting closer. Unable to run any farther, lips dry and struggling for air, she headed for two cotton-woods and collapsed underneath them.

She hadn't seen the caribou. There had to be fifty head, startled by her sudden outburst as they'd come to graze at the waters. With a swift turn of their hides, gray and white fur flapping on shoulders four and five feet off the ground, they turned in perfect syn-chronization, like a troupe of ballet dancers she'd seen once in Seattle, and flew past her.

"Ohh."

The scene was breathtaking.

When her heart finally stopped racing, five min-utes later when the caribou were no longer visible, she wondered if she'd dreamed it. Perhaps she was sleeping still, about to wake up at the fire right beside Quinn, as trapped as she'd ever been.

No. She stroked the firearm in her lap, felt the cold rim of the barrel to convince herself she had escaped.

The whistling had stopped. The pounding of feet, however, grew louder. Perhaps twelve or fifteen yards away in the yellow reeds.

She raised her gun. He was coming closer.

Suddenly beside her, two trumpeter swans squawked through the grasses. What a glorious relief to see them and not him. They had white feathers and dark beaks, and she witnessed the little dance they were doing for each other, wings flapping, oblivious to their human audience.

Just when she was lowering her gun, out came Quinn.

Her heart careened. His attention was glued to the swans to her right. She raised her gun and slid quietly to her feet. The bark of the cottonwood trunk behind her dug into her backside. When he slumped toward the river as if yearning for a cool drink, she pressed her thumb on the hammer and cocked the six-shooter.

The crunch of metal echoed through the reeds and frightened the water birds. They squawked for the second time and dove for the safety of the rushing river.

Quinn, as stunned as the birds, wheeled toward her and lifted his hands slowly. He was panting, sweat at his brow, Stetson tugged low. The fringes on the sleeves of his suede jacket swayed as he raised his arms.

"Autumn…don't be hasty."

"You're through telling me what to do. I shot you once," she said, ignoring that it had been an accident, "so you know I won't hesitate to shoot again. Now…it's your turn to come with me."

"Hand me back my Colt and you won't get hurt." Quinn tried to reason with the crazed woman before this situation got out of hand. He was still shocked from being ambushed moments earlier.

"Ha."

A beam of sunshine hit him between the eyes. His guess was around five o'clock. The sun was rising high above the peaks of the notched mountains—gray and green masses of rock and timber, topped with heaps of ice and snow. The other men had scattered. Quinn doubted they'd even hear him whistle if he tried. He could tackle her, but she was standing too far away. She'd pull the trigger while he was still sailing through the air.

Her blond hair was a mess of scattered leaves, matted with sweat and clumps of blackflies. She was still wearing his long leather duster, unbuttoned down the front. Her red suede skirt had gigantic mud circles at her knees from crawling. Damn, the woman just wouldn't accept that he would take care of her.

He shifted his weight to his other leg, his cowboy boots sinking into the soft grass of the riverbank.

"I…I release you, Autumn. You're free to go."

She laughed aloud, but it was an empty chime. "It's *you* who's trapped by *me*. And you're not free to go."

"I'm stone-tired. You must be, too. Let's call a truce. I'll walk you back and tell the others you're free to go. Doesn't that sound nice?"

"Then why did you follow me?"

"I…feel responsible for your safety."

She frowned.

"I want my gun back."

"Yeah. Sure thing." She rubbed her nose with a sleeve, careful to keep his gun aimed at his face. Son of a bitch, how'd he get into this awful mess?

"Wouldn't you like to put your head down," he asked, "and close your eyes?"

"I'll get enough sleep when I'm dead." She stepped forward, motioning with the gun for him to turn around.

For a timely moment, he didn't budge. But then he noticed the desperate look in her eyes, like a wildcat he'd once accidentally trapped in a barn, and he understood she might very well pull that trigger through instinct, if not reason.

He turned and started hiking along the reeds of the riverbank. "Where to?"

"What's closer? Skagway or the coast?"

Should he tell her the truth? "Skagway."

She scoffed in disbelief behind him. "Then we'll head to the coast."

The coast *was* closer. How did she know he was fibbing?

"You don't want to do this, Autumn."

"Hush."

"You're keeping me from my brother. The poor man is wounded. Don't you have a heart?"

Cold metal jabbed into his ribs. Her voice quavered. "I said hush."

She already knew enough to head west, opposite to the rising sun. On foot like this, they'd reach the coast in two to three hours.

"Is it all right if I put my hands down? It's hard to hold them—"

"No, keep 'em up!"

Another jab to the ribs. She meant business.

Surely she'd tire out soon. Her skirts were heavy, her boots had heels, she was unaccustomed to the wilderness and certainly not as capable as him.

Half an hour later, she was still going strong. Hell. His arms ached from holding them up.

"I wonder how my brother's doing." Quinn tried to let the emotion seep into his voice, to appeal to her sense of decency.

"The others will look after him. They'll take him to that village and find someone to help. I'm sure those were your last orders before you left them."

Damn again.

"In fact, I did your brother a favor by getting everyone up," she said. "He'll be at the village a few hours earlier than expected."

"You've got it all figured out."

"His fever broke. He's breathing easier. Even his color is returning. All the signs we were praying for in my grandpa, that never happened."

"Harrison's fever never broke."

"Huh?"

"It came back. Fever and chills. His breathing is pretty rough again."

"I don't… You're not… *Hush.*"

Decent. Yes, she was decent. And God help him for what he was doing to her.

"You wanted to know how he got stabbed. He was rescuing a family of gold miners. A young couple and their two children. They got jumped by thieves."

"I…I don't care."

"Harrison got in the way of a knife intended for the mother."

"Enough!"

He clamped his lips tight and kept trudging. The riverbank was widening. The swell of the ocean hummed in the far distance. The two mountains they'd been walking between were closing in on them, and the sun was getting stronger on his skin.

"The deputy marshal has sent out a posse," she said, a bit too loud behind him. "They're looking for me. And *you.* I'm sure of it."

"I'm sure of it, too." Quinn's shoulder tensed with the thought. He snatched a look at her expression. Her eyebrows were twisted, as if she were trying to fathom the conversation. He'd give her something to think about.

"Why do you say it like that?" Her skirt swirled about her boots. "You know the man personally?"

"Never met the fella, but I know him."

Her shoulders jarred. "You *know* Deputy Marshal Brander?"

Would she listen to the truth? He braced himself for her reaction. "He's the man who sent the thieves."

Chapter Five

"Why should I believe anything that comes out of your mouth?" Autumn didn't care what the outlaw said about the deputy marshal. She prodded him with the revolver and he, with a heavy sigh, kept walking.

Cool ocean air penetrated her skin as they reached the outskirts of a fishing village, in the early hours of Sunday morning. There was no telling when this man was telling the truth and when he was lying, so there was no sense getting worked up over anything that rolled off his tongue.

Ten feet ahead of her, Quinn slowly swung around to face her. His arms had drifted to his sides a while ago, she suddenly noticed.

"I suppose you shouldn't believe a thing," he said. "You'd be smart not to listen to me at all."

She let out a soft moan of frustration. Every time she thought she knew how to react to this man, he said something that disarmed her.

His lean figure loomed tall among the wild grasses. Suede rippled at his shoulders, his black collar glinted in the slant of the sun's rays and with his dark growth of stubble, he now clearly needed to shave. Birds chirped around them, but she couldn't see them in the leaves, mute witnesses to her misfortune.

"What's the name of this village?"

He peered back to the dozen log houses and shacks that lined a central boardwalk. There was no sign. "Doesn't say, does it?"

"Take your best guess."

"Kirkland."

She searched for a building that looked official— jailhouse, courtroom, anything…but saw none. Maybe she'd see painted letters on one if she drew closer.

His eyes flickered over her gun. She jabbed it higher into the air, letting him know she'd use it if needed.

He seemed to get the message for he took a step back, thumbed the brim of his hat and squinted toward the cabins and the patches of blue water between the buildings. The ocean was barely visible from here. The mountains on either side and the cabins blocked the view.

She shook from the cold. Or maybe fear.

"Is this where they're taking your brother?" she asked.

"Yes."

Lying again? Or not? Autumn deliberated as she studied the stern plane of his cheek. He pulled his lips together.

She swiveled her gaze to the shacks. No one here.

"Where is everyone?" It had to be seven o'clock already. People had to get up to tend to their animals—mules or horses if they had any. Surely goats and chickens. But the lights of the village were out.

He shrugged in reply.

"Keep walking." She nudged his waist from behind, then when he started toward the town, she kept back a safe three yards.

Movement on the ocean caught her attention. There they were. God bless them, they were fishing.

Relief washed over her. Half a dozen little boats bobbed on the waters. Sunlight danced off the blue, blue surface of the inlet, a safe harbor in the Pacific, sandwiched between the glaciers and mountains of Alaska.

She urged Quinn toward a single building at the edge of town, where the rudimentary boardwalk started. Until she figured out who to approach for help, and how to get out of this cat-and-mouse game with this outlaw, she'd keep firm control of the situation with her gun.

The building seemed to be a stage depot of some sort. And likely doubled as a shipping office, for the sign on the corner of the plank building declared Travelers Depot.

Across the street, five buildings down, smoke pumped out of a chimney. In the crackling morning dew, the scent of fresh-brewed coffee wafted their way. A diner.

Autumn and Quinn guzzled a breath of the sweet air at the same time.

She stopped to look at the notice board outside the depot, and came face-to-face with two Wanted posters.

The first one was a man, midthirties, shaggy hair and beard, but with a daring look in his eye that made her gasp. It was him. And there, printed above his head was the confirmation—Quinn Rowlan. Wanted dead or alive for the murder of three fishermen.

Pale and trembling, she turned to the man himself. To the casual observer, he looked nothing like the man in the poster, but she recognized his simmering brown eyes, the tiny mole at the corner of his left eyebrow, the dark brown Stetson.

His face flickered with some sentiment she couldn't read, but then his eyes—those blasted dark eyes—hardened. "That's an old one. I hear the deputy marshal has a newer version in Skagway. Seems I'm wanted for robbing a shipping line of all its gold. And killing the captain."

Her chest constricted. To think she was standing two feet away from a killer. Fearing for her life, she cocked the hammer of her trigger and looked past the other Wanted poster of his men, through the darkened window of the depot, praying there was someone inside who could—

She was startled by Quinn's quick movements. In a flash, he was at her side. He yanked the gun out of her fingers, twisted her wrist in the process and nearly knocked her over. She fell against the railing of the boardwalk.

Horrified, she made to scream, but he clamped his hand over her mouth. She kicked him in the ankle. He groaned, then twisted her arm behind her back till he was almost on top of her.

"Calm down," he said. "Calm down."

Her heart hammered in her throat. Her mouth was dry. Her skin burned from the need to get away. Her muscles ached to run.

"Shh," he said. "Nice and easy. If you calm down, I'll let you go. If you scream, I'll have to take you with me again."

Joined together for a very long stretch of time, her shoulders finally relaxed, and her posture softened.

"Can I take my hand off your mouth? You promise you won't scream?"

She nodded, desperately wondering what would happen now.

His hand eased on her lips, and the one gripping her arm slackened, too. The hard thigh rubbing against hers slid back an inch.

"Someone here will help you get back to Skagway. Nice and slow, now. Easy, easy. This is your chance to be free. Don't blow it. Don't scream."

She nodded.

"If you put up a fuss, I'll have to take you back. Understand?"

She blinked and nodded again, his hand still on the lower part of her jaw.

He released her. His missing gun was already back in its holster. Standing three feet apart like two boxers in a ring, they faced each other. His eyes seemed to glitter with hope and remorse. She stirred with disbelief that he'd let her go.

"Miss Autumn MacNeil…I am sorry." The creases in his face softened, the brown eyes deepened with concern. "I am sorry."

She gulped and nodded. Nodded again and again. Was this finally it? She would have her life back? Free to run or walk or sing or flee? Anticipation soared within her, rushing through her arms and legs.

"Listen, if you need me…" He started to say something, nodding to the direction he was heading, then shook his head as if it were a ridiculous notion. "Take care of yourself. The man who gets *you* is one lucky…"

He didn't finish.

She shoved her hands into her leather pockets.

He strode off the boardwalk, turned his gaze to one side of the deserted main street, then the other, and kept on walking. He was gone from her life as quickly as he'd come.

She stepped forward and gripped the railing. Her hair bobbed across her shoulders.

"Your coat," she whispered weakly, for lack of a better thing to say.

He couldn't have heard at this distance, yet he stopped, swung around, and in one quick sprint, doubled back and jumped up the stairs till he was square in front of her. Breathless at the handsome face inches from hers, Autumn slid the corner of one shoulder out of the duster, but he had other intentions.

"Keep the coat. There's just one more thing."

At the low timbre of his voice, her stomach dropped to her toes. He slid an arm behind her back and crushed her body to his, then his lips thundered down on hers.

She closed her eyes, trapped in his duster, trapped by his hold. Trapped by the intensity of his want of her. She was shocked by the fervor of his mouth, the taste of his moist lips, the hardening, then softening, of his demand.

She felt every hair on the back of her neck as if they were being plucked one by one. Her pulse rumbled in her ears, then came the mad rush of blood to her face, the throbbing of her heart, the warm quiver of desire in her own belly. Such a danger to be in this man's grasp, within reach of…of something deeper in his character.

He kissed as though he'd been caged for a year. Hungry and primal. He slid his large hand behind her duster and up the back of her blouse, resting it just above the waistband where her every cell seemed to connect with his heat. With his other hand he cupped her face, so tantalizingly, such a soft caress in contrast to the firm embrace of her body.

She kissed him back. Perhaps it was *she* who'd been caged for a year. Out-of-control wild.

This wasn't right. She disliked this man.

With a hard push against his firm stomach, she busted free.

Panting, she flashed her lids open, taking in the dark, savage look of a man unglued. The flushed jaw, the slant of black eyebrows, the flared nostrils. He'd lost his hat somewhere in the leap to the boardwalk and so his dark hair tumbled across his forehead, still slicked at the sides from the masquerade ball.

Masquerade. What a joke. She'd been masquerading from him, but in the end, he turned out to be the bigger surprise.

She gripped the lapels of her own coat tighter. "Who are you?"

His jaw stiffened. He peered over her shoulder, not without shame. "The man on the poster." He slowed his breath for a beat and murmured, "And I'm a lawyer."

"What?"

"Studied in Boston."

She searched for the words to tell him how outraged she was by his kiss and this ridiculous lie. How could he be a lawyer? Perhaps he could sense her disbelief, for he lowered his head, scooped his Stetson off the ground and walked away.

A lawyer. It kicked the wind out of her.

He didn't look back this time. She watched his shoulders straighten beneath the suede. The deliberate walk, the confident stride of long legs, and muscles that could pummel any man who stood in his way.

But he had let her go. This vile criminal had wrested the gun from her grip, only to release her in a village of folks who might help her, and had walked straight past a Wanted poster that she could easily point to and scream for justice.

All for the concern over a wounded brother.

She watched him disappear between two buildings. Turning, she stared at his face on the poster, the dark lines the artist had slashed across his jaw, the solemn eyes staring back at her.

Quinn Rowlan. There was more to this man than what was captured on paper.

Still dazed from her release and her last encounter with Quinn, Autumn huddled beneath her bulky leather duster and scooted along the boardwalk, aiming for the safety and serenity of the coffee shack. Lord, she must look a mess. She clawed her fingers through her blond waves as she approached the sign above the log cabin. Clem's Diner, it read. With a push, she burst through the door and was enveloped by the warmth of a roaring grill.

Men. The room was filled with men. Not a feminine wisp of clothing anywhere. A dozen heads turned her way.

"Land's sake, am I dreamin'?" called an older gent with white hair and a fisherman's hat.

Another man, roughly fifty, jumped to his rubber-booted feet. "Mornin', miss."

Another blinked. "Where'd you come from?"

The middle-aged man behind the counter, wearing a white apron from neck to thigh, dried his hands on a towel and approached. Maybe he saw her shaking. "You all right, miss?"

"Yes…yes, I'll be fine. That coffee smells awful nice but I'm afraid I've dropped my wallet and don't have…"

"Coffee for the lady," he shouted. "What's your name?"

"Autumn." She wasn't sure exactly why she withheld her surname, but instinct kept her from talking.

Two younger men, also in rubber boots and fresh black work clothes, nearly knocked heads when they each scrambled to get her a free chair.

The younger one, no more than nineteen with red hair standing straight out on his head as though he'd never combed it this morning, brushed off the wooden seat.

"Thank you." She sank onto pine.

"Take your coat?" asked the other young man. In his early twenties, he had tight blond curls mowed over his ears as though he'd been sheared like a sheep. Something about his dark gaze and predatory manner made her shrink.

"No, no thank you…I prefer to hold tight…"

Fumbling, she rubbed her cheek. Home in Skagway seemed so very far away—the sanctuary of her own bed in the boardinghouse, the comfort of honey and porridge, the refreshing scent of her own laundry…everything.

If her beloved friend Victoria were here, they'd enjoy the attention of these men and maybe even scoot behind the counter and make a show of cooking for them. Or if it were Shaun…he'd hop over the grill and whip up something spectacular—a flaky pastry stuffed with melted cheese. Gilbert was muscled from working in his forge, crafting locks and keys, and he'd require a huge breakfast plate to fuel him. Cornelius was careful of his vocal cords and always asked for tea, not coffee.

"Miss? Glass of water?" the young man asked again.

Autumn tried to concentrate. Someone was speaking to her.

"Yes, please, and if you could spare a roll, I'd be much obliged."

She tried not to pay attention to the looks that passed between these men. Some seemed downright friendly, but others were gaping at her…leering at her body.

No, she shouldn't be so distrustful. Perhaps she was suffering from trauma. The trauma of being kidnapped and then released. Now distrust settled in where it wouldn't normally. These were fine, hardworking gents who could help her.

She shook her head. A lawyer. Then he should know better than anyone that kidnapping was a crime.

She noticed she was being stared at and blurted, "Where are the women?"

The older men chuckled. Three younger ones looked away from her questioning gaze, as though perhaps embarrassed, or pained.

The cook looked up from the grill. Whatever he was cooking smelled like heaven.

The fisherman in the rubber boots brought her coffee, a can of condensed cream and a jar of honey. Oh, the joy. She dug in.

"There's forty-two men in this village. We ain't seen a female since last year, when Clem's daughter and her husband came through. Most folks push on to the Klondike."

Clem had to be the cook, for he looked up and nodded.

"It's a difficult journey," she said. She understood how hard it was, especially for women if they had young children, or older folks to attend. And if two women alone wanted to make this journey, Lord help them from being accosted on the trail. Women had to be well-armed and unafraid to use their weapons.

She savored her first sip of coffee, but something—a hand—patted the back of her head. Startled, she turned around. Good heavens, the sheep-sheared young man was fondling her hair.

She pulled away.

"Brooks!" Clem hollered.

Some men coughed in embarrassment.

When a plate of food was brought to her table, every male eye in the room stopped to watch her eat. She chomped on the warm biscuit while forking the grilled halibut.

"Been a long year since I last saw my wife," said the hollow-cheeked man sitting across from her.

Her coat had parted to reveal her blouse and he

was staring straight at her chest. She clenched her lapels together in alarm.

"I like the sound of your voice," said the barrel-chested man who smelled like moss sitting next to her. "Could you please talk some more?"

"I'm headed to Skagway," she said between paranoid gulps. "Anyone going that way?"

Six or seven men lunged forward. The shouting jarred her ears.

"I saw her first!"

"I can get you there fast!"

"Let's make a deal!"

And then it all spun out of control. Panic quaked through her body as the adolescent punched the twentysomething. The man who hadn't seen his wife for a year jumped over the table and grabbed her shoulders, making her horror multiply. The old fisherman in the rubber boots tried to bust up the fight.

Clem stood up on a chair and banged on his pots, shouting, "Calm down! You bunch of idiots!"

Autumn tried to wrestle free of the despicable man, the wayward husband who'd slipped his hand to her breast. Yuck. When he wouldn't let go, she kneed him hard between the legs. He howled. Others were still shouting, the banging got louder and the crash of glass echoed in her ears as she ran for the door and hurled herself back to the safety of the street.

Where in thunder was her lawyer?

Chapter Six

An hour later on the other side of the village, Quinn watched the old captain cut into Harrison's infected gut. Unable to witness the visceral display, Quinn sat on the cot beside his brother and turned his face to the floorboards. He winced at his younger brother's growls of agony.

"Easy," Quinn murmured. He gripped Harrison's sweaty hand. The other men were eating breakfast in the adjoining room, at his insistence, getting ready to head out again.

"Almost done," bellowed Captain Bird. A pudgy man with spectacles, a square head and gray temples, he worked quickly. "Done this once before. Drained an abscess on a sailor's knee on the way from Cape Horn. Terrible storm. Waves as tall as St. Peter's, I swear. Saved the leg. Couldn't prevent a limp."

"We're grateful for your help." Staring at the floor,

Quinn winced again as he heard a twist of medical scissors and sutures.

"Uh," muttered Harrison. The captain had said he didn't know how to draw up a syringe of morphine from Autumn's medical bag, but they'd given him another swig of laudanum. Harrison's fever had returned, but hopefully with the draining, they might turn a corner.

Staring at the opened medical bag, Quinn shuffled his big boots across the floor and wondered whose it was. Autumn had told him its location at the masquerade ball, so it likely belonged to one of the nurses in town, one of her friends.

He wished Autumn well, and knew that any man in this town would trip over himself to help her. All she had to do was ask.

She was likely on her way to Skagway this very minute. Back to her home, her friends, her beaux—of which there were plenty, Quinn was sure—and her fancy lotions and ball gowns. A world of wealth and class he'd never been privy to, growing up as a rancher's son, but he'd entered that world on occasion while he'd studied criminal law in the upper ranks of Boston. Not much of a rancher, his pa—who was by trade an office clerk from Boston who'd made his way west—but the man was a model in how he'd run his life. He always kept his word and never took advantage of a neighbor.

Quinn looked back to the stitched wound as Captain Bird wrapped gauze around Harrison's ribs. Just as Autumn had predicted, the captain had left a cotton wick hanging out of the incision *and* the bandaging, in order for any remaining pus to drain.

"You gotta change the bandages and soak the area with antiseptic. Once or twice a day, if you got the supplies."

"We got 'em." Quinn explained to his groggy brother, "We're sitting next to the ocean. There must be a ship a week that crosses this way. I'm sending you back to North Dakota."

"Like…hell…"

"You could buy back the ranch and—"

"Like hell! What good is a name," Harrison growled from the bed, "if you can't stand behind it."

"I'll clear our name. You've got to rest and—"

"What're you gonna do? Tie me up in the apple tree like you used to?"

Captain Bird rose, walked to a nearby stand and washed his hands in the basin. "Problems, mister?"

"Got my fair share." Quinn stood up and reached into his pocket for his suede pouches that carried his gold. He removed a generous nugget and placed it on the night table. "Much obliged, Captain."

The man nodded and addressed Quinn by the phony names he'd given earlier. "Jim and John Windsor."

Turning back to Harrison, who had his eyes closed, Quinn debated what to do. He could leave his brother here overnight, but they'd be taking their chances—

Footsteps and the slamming of the front door interrupted his thoughts. He pulled his gun and slid to the bedroom door to look into the kitchen.

It was her. *Autumn.* His pulse hammered. Where had she come from? Her hair billowed like a lion's mane around her face. Her eyes bulged in panic. She looked desperately around the room, trying to locate something. Him.

Quinn stepped forward but as she jumped toward him, Jackson leaped up from the breakfast table and tackled her waist.

"What in tarnation are you doin' here?" asked Jackson.

"Quinn! I need to see Quinn!"

"Jim? Jim's right here." Jackson gritted his teeth at her. She knew enough to keep quiet at the odd name. And so far, she hadn't blurted that Quinn's face was on a Wanted poster ten doors down. Maybe he could trust her. Maybe. She turned to face Quinn at the bedroom door.

"Let her go," he rumbled.

Jackson did so, and Autumn, panting and shoving strands of loose hair from her sweaty temples, took a moment to catch her breath. Her face was red, her eyes watering and her nose tinged by the cold. Agitated and twisting her fingers together, she looked through the front window panes of the cabin. Quinn followed her troubled gaze and spotted two young men, one fair haired and scrawny, the other a red-haired brute. The two were shuffling their feet and passing a cigarette between them.

Quinn turned his sights back on the flustered damsel. "Found someone to help you?"

"Very helpful. Yes, very helpful indeed. Wonderful town." She glanced past Quinn's shoulder to the captain. "Everyone wanting to do so much for me."

"I'm pleased to hear it," said Quinn. "How'd you find me?"

"I asked around for who might know something about medicine in this town."

"Ma'am," said Captain Bird behind him, "I'd be honored if you joined us for breakfast. Haven't had a woman here since…well, I've never had a woman here."

"Thank you, Captain, but I've eaten already."

She obviously knew the man was a captain, thought Quinn. "They treat you well over at Clem's?"

"You would not believe it."

Enough of this pleasant hogwash. Quinn had serious matters to attend to, and she seemed to have settled things well enough on her own.

"What do you need?" He stepped forward and whispered as Jackson, Vic, Trevor and Ben rose from the table to make room for the remaining two men who hadn't yet eaten—Quinn and the captain. Quinn took Autumn at her word—she'd had breakfast and wasn't hungry. He wasn't going to offer again. Ah, the thought hit. "Need some gold? For your travels?"

"It could help." She gulped.

His mouth watered at the scent of boiled ham from a tin, but still, he found it difficult to sit down and eat with a lady standing.

"Your brother?" She peered across his shoulders on tiptoe.

"Taken care of. Sleeping now."

"Good. Very good."

She took the teeny gold nugget Quinn offered and kept her hand out for more. Just how much did he owe this woman? He placed another nugget in her palm. She still didn't lower her hand. He tucked his tongue into the pocket of his cheek and showed her that his pouch was empty. Nothing but flakes left. She didn't need to know about the other pouches.

"Yes, well, thank you," she said briskly. "Doesn't quite square us up, though, does it?"

Quinn squinted. "How's that again?"

A sharp pounding on the wooden door caused her to jump in alarm.

"I mean you owe me. It's your duty to return me to Skagway. Right this very minute."

Quinn studied the serious turn of her face for a moment, then his grin mingled with the laughter of the other men in the room. He sat down at the table and grabbed a slice of rye bread. The boys at the door were still banging to get in. They were waiting as politely as they knew how.

"Sure you don't want a cup of coffee or anything?" Quinn asked her between bites. The bread was stale, but Lord, delicious.

She shook her head and pinched her lips together. Her cheeks grew redder.

The captain joined Quinn at the table. He quirked

an eyebrow at Autumn, then winked at Quinn. "Now she's a problem I wouldn't mind having."

Quinn was reminded of their heated kiss, although he didn't let on. A meeting of mouths that left him rumbling for more.

Jackson opened the door to the banging and stepped outside to investigate the commotion. Quinn heard a lot of mumbling, then Jackson reached for his gun. The two young men scrambled away.

The men outside weren't so friendly after all. Had she been in some sort of trouble?

Autumn let out a huge sigh at the sight of their disappearing backs. Her shoulders fell, the tight lines around her mouth softened.

"You best be heading out now, if you want to make it home by tomorrow," he said, prodding her.

His comment lit a fire in her brown eyes. She whipped into the empty chair beside him. Quinn signaled to Vic to start moving out, and the men did as he asked. Two hustled into the other room, with Vic packing the food items they'd bought from the captain.

Vic distracted Captain Bird with questions to give Quinn a moment with Autumn. "Say, Captain Bird, how did you come to be in Alaska?" Vic asked.

Irritated at having to look away from Autumn's pretty face, the captain explained his story to Quinn's man.

Meanwhile, Autumn stuck her elbow into Quinn's. "Now you listen here, *Jim*."

Quinn couldn't help but laugh. Her tactics were useless.

She lowered her voice to a hush. "I could tell the captain a thing or two about your...real name."

Quinn stopped laughing. "You wouldn't dare."

"Why not?"

"Because for some reason," he said, "you don't like this village. And if you opened your mouth about anything, you'd be stuck here."

She tapped her chin. "The captain's nice. He'd help me out of my jam."

"Then go ahead and ask him," Quinn said, calling her bluff.

She stared at Quinn. Her facial muscles flickered as though deliberating what to do. On edge, she fiddled with her hands, then looked up and studied Vic, who was rolling up smoked salmon in sheets of old newspapers. Then she flashed her long brown lashes at the sea captain.

"Oh, Captain," she called, leaning across Quinn—dammit, close enough for him to whisper into her hair—to press her hand on the captain's sleeve.

The old man accidentally dropped his bread on the plate in anticipation. If he'd had a tail, he would've been wagging it like a dog waiting to be petted.

"You've helped these men a lot," she began.

At her threat of disclosure, Quinn's men appeared around them. Vic slyly took out his gun, Ben strode in from the other room and Trevor thumbed his holster. All done without the captain even noticing the silent threat. If she tried to reveal who they were, she wouldn't get far.

Autumn gulped at the faces. If she put them in any danger, they'd take the necessary precautions and pull her out of there. Fast. Defeated, she slumped back in her chair.

"Thank you, Captain, for taking care of…of my friends." Whatever she was threatening to say, to disclose about Quinn and his gang, went unsaid.

And that's when the guilt settled in on Quinn.

Hell, why should he feel so bad about this woman? Quinn had known all along she was never in any real danger from him, so he shouldn't feel like scum on a pond.

What about the good things he and his men had accomplished? The folks they'd protected on the trail, the sleepless nights they'd spent tracking down Brander's men, the knife wound Harrison had taken in the gut? That counted for something, didn't it?

Yet, as he watched Autumn remove her coat to reveal that lacy white blouse that clung to her curves, and then solemnly sip her coffee while the captain patted her arm and stroked her back in a sickening gesture of proximity, Quinn was consumed by a mystifying rage.

Why did he have to deal with other people's problems all the blasted time?

Why wasn't he free to pat her arm and stroke her pretty face?

The captain stood up and walked to the window.

He leaned back against a cabinet and crossed his arms. "Miss Autumn," he drawled.

She frowned. "Yes?"

"Miss Autumn MacNeil."

Her cheeks blistered. Quinn zeroed in on the man's face. What was this now? How did the old guy know her surname?

The captain stroked his whiskered jaw. "Your looks confused me. Last time I saw you, your hair was all braided up and you were wearing a brown lace dress."

Quinn lowered his fork and rose to the door.

Autumn looked down at the floorboards as she jumped up, perhaps trying to avoid the attention.

But the captain couldn't be stopped. "You do sing like an angel."

Quinn wondered what that meant.

"Prettiest singer in Skagway. You still at the Imperial Hotel?"

"Yes, well, sometimes." She reached for the doorknob and pulled. "I...I need a breath of fresh air. Thank you for the coffee."

She was out the door and on the porch before Quinn could get a word in.

He'd never pictured her as an entertainer. He'd pictured her as...as coming to Alaska to hook up with a rich gold miner, or maybe a shrewd businessman. She'd said she worked in the hotel, but he'd figured maybe as a chambermaid.

Quinn eased his shoulders through the tight doorway

and joined her on the porch. He inhaled fresh mountain air. "I didn't know you were talented that way."

She slid her arms into her coat again. He stepped forward to help, but she was so fast, she did it without him and he was left feeling awkward. And that damn guilt again.

"Good luck with your brother," she said.

"Thanks." Was this to be her exit, then? He watched her studying the streets. For signs of what?

"Would you mind terribly… I promise not to use it on you— Would you mind giving me one of your guns? I would feel…I would feel more…"

With a roll of his head, he looked to the sky and exhaled. How could he leave a woman in distress? No one had ever helped his ma in time, when she had needed it. He had only been twelve years old when he went to the livestock auction with her that day. Two men had been arguing over the price of ten heads of cattle, it had escalated into a fistfight and ended with an accidental gunshot into his mother's back.

Nothing Quinn could've done to save her.

But there was an awful lot he could do to protect this one.

It shamed him to know that maybe he'd been acting the same as those two men at the auction, so wrapped up in their personal misery over the price of cattle that they hadn't noticed the young mother bidding on chickens with her son. Only in this case, Quinn had been wrapped up with Harrison.

Harrison, however, had survived the stabbing.

"I can't give you my gun."

Her expression fell. She restrained her anger, but it was evident in the cusp of her upper lip. "I see. Well…thank you for the gold. I imagine I could trade it for a weapon someplace in town."

She stepped off the porch, heading to the shops again, then stopped and swung around to Quinn. "I'm not sure what's going on between you and the deputy marshal, but…I will be notifying him."

Was she giving him some warning? Was she telling him for his own good, to stay out of Skagway? Or was it a self-protective stance, telling him to stay away from her?

But the nagging guilt—that sense of right and wrong and the need to justify his actions to her, to show her he wasn't all bad—drove him.

"Hang on," he said, voice dropping. He jumped off the porch step to landed at her skirts. "Dammit, I'll take you home."

Chapter Seven

Autumn was having a hard time understanding this man who came from nowhere. Thirty minutes after Quinn had agreed to escort her home, she was preparing to saddle up while his men were shouldering into position beneath the trees, still trying to convince Quinn he was making a grave mistake. She wondered if what he had implied about the deputy marshal held any truth, then what parts of his explanations should she believe? *Could* she believe?

If Quinn truly was a lawyer, then his situation went deeper than merely personal. If the deputy marshal was falsely accusing him of criminal activities, then Quinn couldn't practice law, either. His very livelihood was at stake.

Truth be told, she didn't rightly wish to hear any of his explanations. They were *his* problems. Her problem was getting home, as fast and furiously from these outlaws—or whoever they were—as possible.

But as she listened to his men's pleadings, her stomach quelled like an ocean storm.

"How can you go with her?" Jackson craned his neck around Quinn's Stetson to glare at Autumn as she stood patting the Appaloosa, her fingers shaking on the soft, spotted coat.

The horse snorted and she jumped. Still not used to the big beast.

"My detour shouldn't hamper us," Quinn answered. "You go on with Harrison to the location—" he looked her way and she snapped back to her saddle, pretending she wasn't listening "—we agreed on. We'll set the plan in motion for Brander."

"Without you?"

"We'll be out of touch two days. Three at most. I know where you're headed and I *will* find you."

"But *you're* headed straight into the fire."

"I'll be all right. Brander was at the masquerade ball and he didn't recognize me off the poster, what with my new haircut. If I run into him or any of his men, I'm safe."

"It's her you have to worry about. She'll turn you in first chance she gets."

"Somehow I don't believe that. I think she'll keep her mouth shut if I get her home safe."

Unsure of what she would do, and irritated that he would assume the best of her, Autumn stuffed the items she'd received from the captain—an extra canteen and food seasonings—into a saddlebag. Knowing she was being watched, she forced a positive expression on her face and pretended Quinn didn't have anything to worry about in her.

But he *did*. She had to tell someone what was going on. Her friends. Or maybe Brander himself.

Quinn muttered something more, but she couldn't make it out. She heard the thud of his heavy footsteps on the wet grass, and suddenly he was beside her.

He touched her wrist and she inhaled a barrel of air. "You'll have Harrison's horse this time."

"By myself?" Autumn turned to the golden mare hitched beside the four other horses.

"Think you can handle it?"

"Um… You'll ride slow, won't you?"

"Couldn't gallop for long even if we tried. The shrubs are thick and there's barely a path."

She nodded and he helped her up into the saddle. Their fingers slid together and she was reminded of his embrace earlier. The pressure of his lips, the seductive way he'd kissed her. The leather saddle squeaked as she arranged her skirt. The horse snorted and turned its head. She stilled as quiet as a mouse in captivity, scared out of her wits for having to handle the huge horse on her own. But the mare settled as Quinn rose in his horse, and her tense muscles loosened.

Still on her guard, she rode out with Quinn. She waved to the captain, but not to any of the other men since they weren't looking too friendly.

Quinn led, and soon they were riding along the riverbank, its waters raging with the newly melted ice of spring. She simmered along with the gurgling, her nerves racing for several reasons—she was alone with Quinn, unaccustomed to her mare's size and anxious for what and who awaited her in Skagway.

It would be a pleasure to embrace her friend Victoria, to tell her all that had passed. An unbelievable story, really. Who had she missed most from her male friends? Gilbert's friendly laugh and the muscled hands of a man who made his living as a locksmith? The gentleness of Shaun's grin when he was lost in his baking? Or all she had in common with Cornelius, the baritone who sang beside her at the Imperial?

As he rode ahead of her, Quinn didn't feel much like talking. This was fine with her, for she would rather not get to know him. He'd drop her off on the outskirts of Skagway, and if she were fortunate, they would never see each other again.

Instead of dwelling on the negative aspects of this whole situation, her mind wandered to the positive, and what she'd say to old Mr. Dirkson, manager of Skagway's Credit and Loan, at four o'clock tomorrow.

She'd be frank about her skills as a shopkeeper, give her forecast for growing the business. She'd tell him her plans for introducing one of those popular gift shops for knickknacks and small treasures, perhaps photos of the entertainers that customers loved to collect. Lotions for women and imported fabrics. She'd nurture her business slowly but steadily, and aimed to have the biggest and most lucrative hotel in all of Alaska.

"You hungry?" Quinn turned in his saddle and called back to her, well past noon. His black shirt tugged at his shoulders. His brown hat framed the angular profile of his face.

"Yeah."

"Got some jerky in my pack."

They also shared biscuits and a tin of corn.

The afternoon passed with barely another snort from Quinn, but she found it strangely pleasing that he turned his back on her as they rode. It was a level of trust she hadn't anticipated, that he wasn't afraid she'd pull a knife or a gun on him, if she'd gotten her hands on one.

But she still didn't trust *him* fully. How could she? She was eager to get home, but she wasn't stupid.

However, as the horse swayed beneath her skirts, that kiss burned in her thoughts. The hot memory of his mouth on hers. What an unexpected move he'd made; selfish and…and primitive…and the same as what so many other men had often tried at the hotel. Why did men always want the same thing?

To occupy her mind as her mare made its way through the pines and dunes of the tidal flats, she hummed one of her favorite tunes.

Hours later, the sky was still filled with the sun when it was time to bed down.

"You handled your horse just fine," Quinn told her around the campfire.

She'd long ago removed her duster, and so stood simply in blouse and skirt as she unpacked. "I pretended she was a mule, only bigger."

For some reason, he thought this humorous. The gentle creases around his eyes gave depth to his amusement. Her eyes dropped to the mouth that had kissed her.

Flushing, she turned away quickly, pulled one of the saddlebags closer and rummaged through it.

"What're you looking for?"

"A…brush or a comb. My hair's in knots."

He rose to full intimidating height and extracted something from his pack. "I've got one to lend."

His black comb had thin bristles. She doubted she could get it through her tangles, but would try. "Thank you."

She brought it up to the left side of her head, but it jammed above her ear.

"Try it down lower," he suggested, standing in front of her. "Work your way up."

What did he know about combing out long hair? How terribly intimate to imagine him brushing a woman's hair.

But as his cinnamon-brown eyes flashed back at hers, she knew in her belly he'd done this before. He'd combed out *some* woman's hair. He'd likely bathed a back or two, and undressed plenty, unprincipled man that he was.

His gaze lowered down her face. His hand came up and caressed her cheek.

She froze from the shock of his warm hand. There was a charm to him this evening, a glint of vulnerability she hadn't seen before. The thread of attraction between them was undeniable. It was a pounding energy, a friction that ignited like flint to fire.

He lowered his hand and turned away before she could see what more was in his eyes.

She breathed a heavy sigh of relief.

Taking her canteen, partially full of water, she sat on the opposite side of the fire, pretending as though she wasn't aware of the lightning that had just passed between them. She carefully wet the ends of her hair and continued passing the comb through it.

From bottom to top, as he'd suggested.

She'd felt this sort of tension before. There'd been a man she'd left behind in Seattle. He'd helped her forget her loneliness, if only for a brief few hours. Those were details she didn't dwell on, or perhaps didn't want to admit, but oh, how she'd buried herself in the sinful pleasures of the flesh as she mourned the loss of her grandparents.

Had it been so wrong? To be wanted and chased and kissed? To feel someone else's heart pounding next to hers, to let her know she was alive and desirable?

Older folks would likely damn her. Her face prickled with a thousand barbs. She saw herself as imperfect. Troubled then, but less prone to fall for that sort of thing now. She was stronger, and holding out for a future more secure and loving, not a brief interlude that left her empty when all had been said and done.

Here with Quinn, she felt all those same raging emotions—the desire pounding through her bloodstream, the need for contact, the urge to kiss and be kissed. She was a strong, healthy woman, and he was equally in his prime. The feelings were natural. It was the urge to act on them she had to suppress.

"When you get back to Skagway, I would appreciate it if you don't mention my name for twenty-four hours."

She stopped combing and watched him remove his fishing tackle. "Twenty-four?"

"I'm hoping, of course, that you'll never mention my name. But if you find you can't stop yourself…I'd be mighty obliged if you gave me a chance to get my men to safety first."

She toyed with the comb in her fingers, waiting and wondering what to do about him.

"Harrison's a good man. He was trying to help a stranger when he got stabbed," he said.

"So you keep saying."

"Brander will be the first to come calling on you."

"How do you know that?"

"It's his pattern."

"How do you know his pattern?"

"It's what he's been doing for the last year and a half."

"Why don't you confront him? Why don't you tell everyone you meet your story, convince them Brander's a criminal and have him arrested?"

"Tried that six months ago."

"And?"

"When he found out his two deputies were willing

to give evidence against him, he killed them. One had a family back in Philadelphia."

She shuddered.

Patting off her red suede skirt, she rose to her feet. "I don't need to hear this. You must've done something wrong for the law to come after you. I've met plenty of your kind. I hear them at the hotel while they're playing cards. How someone else tricked them out of their money. How the bottles of whiskey they consume affect everyone else's judgment but their own. How the gold that their neighbor struck should have rightly been theirs. I'm so tired of hearing stories. Please."

"Think back," he said. "Six months ago. What happened to Deputies Mason and Zale?"

She frowned. "They went ice fishing...."

"When did they return?"

She gulped. "No one has made mention.... I thought they moved on.... They were fishermen and hunters who were just filling in as temporary lawmen."

"If you have the inclination, ask Brander what happened to them."

With that bold suggestion, Quinn took his fishing tackle and headed through the trees and down the banks of the river.

Why did she care so much about engaging this man? What was it that was drawing her attention, her sympathy to his plight? It surely couldn't be good for her.

"I don't care about his problems," she whispered

into the glowing evening sky. But her pulse beat against her flesh as she watched his muscled frame disappear over the grassy slopes.

Quinn wasn't going to let the woman affect him. Who cared whether she believed him or not? He knew the truth. But his temper flared and his muscles hardened every time he looked into those innocent round eyes.

Forget her…forget her…forget her. Quinn unraveled his fishing line off the spool, baited the end with a worm he'd dug up in the moist grass and tossed it into the clear blue water.

He was ambushed by the memory of that awful night a week ago….

Quinn raised his hand and gave a signal for his men behind him to proceed with caution. He plunged his oar over the side of the canoe and headed for the disturbing noises on the riverbank. The midnight sun blazed above his shoulders, but he couldn't enjoy the serenity of his surroundings.

"What is it?" The whisper came from Harrison, seated in the rear of the canoe.

Quinn had heard it, too. Raised voices, hammers cocking in the woods ahead. He lifted his hand again, and the three canoes, filled with six wanted men, came to a sudden stop in the waters.

Someone was being overrun on the trail.

The lapping of beaver tails echoed from farther upstream. Quinn lifted his oar to indicate each canoe to go in a different direction. The men did so without question.

He and Harrison arrived first.

They spotted the married couple on their knees, guns drawn to their temples, then the two adolescent daughters—twins—huddled together and crying beneath the shadow of seven scruffy men glaring at them like hungry scavengers.

A chest full of gold nuggets sat askew at the campfire.

Many would call this family, these gold miners, lucky. Lucky to have struck treasure when thousands of others had failed. But Quinn had seen this sight of robbery so often, he wondered whether any newfound wealth was worth it.

Brander's hired men.

Hiding behind the great cedars along the bank, Quinn nodded at his younger brother. They slid their guns from their holsters, pointed carefully and fired. They blasted the two men who were threatening the couple, two more who were closing in on the young girls for a different vile act, and three more who were cursing and running for their horses.

Seconds later when his men arrived to help, Quinn ran and fell to his knees beside the woman. "You all right?"

She moaned. No wounds visible. "My baby girls…"

"They're fine, ma'am. They're fine."

Her husband, sprawled on the grass beside his wife, gripped his six-shooter, rolled to his stomach and aimed between the trees at the fleeing men.

"No," Quinn shouted, "let my men handle—"

Too late. One of Brander's men jumped toward the woman, knife drawn. Harrison lunged to protect her and got in the way of the blade.

Struck by an icy panic, Quinn blasted a bullet in the man's direction, nicked him in the wrist, but he escaped, running like a coward to his horse.

Quinn raced to Harrison's side. "Don't move. Don't move."

"Go after 'em," Harrison groaned.

"Let me have a look." The damage was intense. Skin flapped above his ribs, a hole the size of a snowball. Quinn tugged the bandanna off his neck and cupped it firmly over the bleeding. Harrison yelped.

"We need a doctor."

His brother flinched. "None around."

"I'll get someone," Quinn vowed.

"Leave me behind if you need to."

"Never." When the shooting faded, when his men secured the area and helped the travelers to their feet, when Quinn counted four of the seven dead but three who got away, he ordered Harrison be lifted into the canoe.

"Don't know about movin' him," said Jackson.

"We'll bury the dead and escort the family to safety. Then some of us'll head to Skagway."

"Skagway? We'll be shot on sight."

"He needs a doctor."

Jackson didn't argue further and followed command as Quinn helped lift his groaning brother.

Quinn no longer recalled how he'd come to be in command, only that he was. He stared at his brother's now-unconscious body. In the many years they'd spent together on the plains of North Dakota, terror gripped Quinn as it never had before....

A tug on his fishing line brought Quinn back to his present problems. Recovering from the heart-heavy memory, he channeled his thoughts to reeling in a black bass. Its fins gleamed in the night sun. It'd be enough food for the two of them. He gutted it at the river and headed back to the fire.

He found her rinsing her blouse. A bar of glycerin soap sat beside her canteen, and she was spot-cleaning the dirt stains on her chest. Circular wet patches on the white lace fabric adhered to the red corset beneath. Her bosom was curvaceous, her waistline so slender before the gentle swell of her hips.

He'd never seen anything so beautiful in all his life.

Most moving of all, she was singing "Amazing Grace." Her voice was deeper than he expected, reso-nating through the hushed air of the forest, as if the birds and insects themselves were listening. It stirred a deep part of Quinn he didn't wish stirred. As the melody and the words reached his ears and ripped through his heart, all it did was remind him of things he'd lost and things he couldn't have.

Chapter Eight

Quinn's movements were so loud, his boots crackling on the twigs beside her, that Autumn started out of her song.

"Don't let me stop you," he grumbled, setting his filet in the pan and seating himself on a log across from the fire. "Sing all you want."

But his irritated voice said the contrary. He wasn't pleased with her singing.

Her pulse was still pounding from the unexpected interruption. Self-conscious, she looped her towel over her shoulders, trying to conceal the wet stains on her blouse.

He seemed to be avoiding a glance in her direction and was fixated on his fish. She'd never had such a disinterested audience. Not that she'd been singing for him; the song had slipped out without her noticing.

By the grim set to his jaw and the pressured line of his lips, he obviously preferred silence. Or perhaps the sounds of the night forest. The whistling of wet wood in the roaring fire, the hoot of night owls, the swoosh of the river in the distance.

She braced her knees and responded to nature's beauty, too. Smoke tinged her nostrils, but the scent of frying fish and the sight of his large, muscled hands turning it over in the fire mesmerized her. The orange flames heated all the parts of her closest to the fire—her nose, her mouth, her knees and her knuckles. It sunk into her bones and muscles and relaxed her like no amount of whiskey or singing could.

"Tired?" he asked, several minutes later. He finally looked up and met her eyes.

"I didn't think I was. Until I sat down."

"That's what it's like on the trail."

"Ever get an urge to stay in one place?"

"I get it all the time."

She strained forward. Then why didn't he...?

There was no need to answer the question. He couldn't stop to rest until he set his life in order. Squared things up with the deputy marshal.

"Prove to me you're a lawyer."

He thought about it. "I studied with the famous Professor Thomas B. Anthony Muller."

"You could've made that up. I don't know that name."

He thought some more. "The Declaration of Independence was adopted by Congress on July 4, 1776."

"Plenty of people know that."

"Edward Rutledge was the youngest one to sign it. Age twenty-six. Benjamin Franklin was the oldest. Seventy."

"Hmm," she said, still unconvinced. "That could've been a lucky guess."

"Lucky guess?" He peered over the fire at her, pretending as though he were wounded.

She shrugged, unwilling to commit.

"Let's see…the Sixth Amendment to the United States Constitution guarantees the criminal defendant the right to a speedy and public trial, heard by an impartial jury. He has the right to be informed of the nature and cause of the accusation, the right to be confronted with the witnesses against him. And also has the right to Legal Counsel in his defense. The Fifth Amendment states he shall not be deprived of life, liberty or property without due process of the law…."

"Blazes," she whispered. It was true.

He stopped talking. Fire reflected on his face, the nubs on his jaw and the slant of his cheekbones. It even painted his short lashes golden. "You're starting to believe me."

It was hard to give in to his smile of satisfaction. "No, I'm not."

"Yeah, you are." It was a full-blown grin now, warm and lazy.

She resisted his masculine charms. "No, I don't believe one word of what you say."

He arched his brows. "I don't see you reaching for any guns."

"That's different…you gave your word."

"See what I mean? You're taking me at my word."

"I am not!"

"There's just the two of us here. I won't tell anyone you've got some affection for me."

"I *do* not!"

"Good-looking fella like me? Who can wrestle a bass out of the water in five minutes flat, ride a horse for a week straight and recite the Constitution?"

"Is your brother as vain as you?"

"Much worse."

"Then…I…I wish you much happiness together."

"Thank you." His eyes glistened. "See, there you go again. Paying me a compliment."

She fought the smile tugging at her mouth. Turning away from him and the fire, she jumped to her feet.

"I'll get the plates!"

She found them in a saddlebag, along with two scratched forks. Making her way back to his side for him to divvy up the portions, she was grateful for the towel that covered her bosom and the clump of wet hair that fell against her cheeks, masking his full view of her face, in case he saw the growing respect there.

He removed the fish off the heat and set the pan on a flat boulder between them. She thrust out the plates, the towel around her neck swaying around her bosom. "Ready."

"Are you?"

He reached up and pushed the hair from her cheek,

his fingertips grazing her flesh, the heat of her reaction bolting straight through to her thighs.

She felt trapped, holding the plates while he was touching her, silly for being outsmarted…facing temptation and not knowing how to handle it. Handle him.

She caught his gaze straight-on. The flecks of light reflecting in his eyes from the fire contrasted with the deep intensity of his pupils, the bronze flavor of his cheeks, the wild stroke of his finger on her throat. His touch ignited her like a match to paper.

"Such beauty," he murmured.

She trembled there in her boots, in her draping suede skirt and the corset that seemed to tighten around her ribs, restricting her ability to breathe.

He slid the plates from her grasp, as if she were too stuck to move. Then he simply dropped them to the grass, not even bothering to care where they fell. And still her stomach churned. Every part of her came alive with the scent of Quinn, the awareness that his mouth was a feather away from hers, that her heart was knocking inside her chest and her legs were trembling with the thought of flight.

She didn't run.

He cupped the back of her neck, weaving his warm fingers into her damp hair, and pulled her that last inch forward to close the agonizing gap between them.

His chest met hers. His mouth touched hers. The heat of their union melted them into one.

It was a soft promise of what might be, if she'd let

him. His mouth tugging on hers, his breath pounding through her, the fever of his wants transparent.

And her own. She reached up and stroked his neck. He moaned and kissed one side of her mouth, then the other, then came fully down on her lips, pressing his thighs into hers, letting her know how much she aroused him. She broke free, her face throbbing.

Quinn stared down at the pretty woman in his arms, her face tilted upward to his, her breathing vigorous and uneven, the firm swell of her bosom pressed into his ribs. Her brown eyes flicked in the dimming light, the fire's fingers blazing the side of her cheeks.

"I won't hurt you," he promised.

"Ohh…"

He didn't wait to hear more. He kissed the slender hollow of her creamy throat, marveling at its softness. How could anything so soft exist? He slid the towel from around her neck and let it fall to the ground.

He undid one button at her neckline, then another and another. She resisted, bringing her fingers up to stop his, but he persisted and, with a heavy groan, she allowed him the pleasure. When he reached the last button—twenty-two blasted pearl beads in all, for he'd been counting from the hour they'd met—he gave her blouse a tug to yank out the tail, and it opened, like a velvet curtain onstage, to reveal the most remarkable show.

Red lace cups gripped her waist. Whalebone and straps and crisscrossed stays. Almost spilling out of the top of her red satin cups were breasts so smooth and voluptuous they stole his breath. And made him rock hard.

Perhaps feeling suddenly overwhelmed, she tried to snatch her blouse closed, but he wouldn't allow it, tugging the cloth open.

"Please…let me look at you…let me look…."

Not wanting to break the spell, wanting to remember its captivation always, he trailed a finger along the top of her cleavage, the top of one golden breast, down the valley and over to the other. He could feel she was affected. She sucked in some air, shuddered in a feminine sigh, and then came that gentle, almost imperceptible tilt toward him that indicated her consent.

He circled her waist with both hands, kissed the top of her left breast and with a gentle tug, yanked down her cups.

She gasped but he kept going, his gaze clinging to her body. Large pink areolae, flat and soft in the firelight and as big as two plums, beckoned for his mouth. He pressed his lips to one and then the other, wetting the nipples, making them glisten in the firelight. He flicked his tongue around the edge of one areola, then played with the other until she couldn't seem to stand it any longer and gripped the side of his head, fingers entwining his hair.

He wanted to please her. Swinging her up and over, he laid her down to his bedroll. All the while kissing her breasts, her throat, the swell of her underarm and back to her throat.

He found her hot mouth again.

With a fever that seemed equal to his own, she kissed him and undid the buttons of his shirt. With a slight hesitation, they clawed their way into each other's clothing, she helping to undo his fly, he eager to yank off her pantaloons, till they were a mishmash of twisted cloth and bare skin.

"You are something to behold," he murmured, so hard and ready he felt as though he might explode.

She rolled a shoulder beneath his blanket and pressed against his hand as he led himself lower to her private parts, gripping her buttock. He explored her thighs, her knee, down one calf, and after several hushed minutes, he slipped his fingers back up her thighs and against her center.

Their eyes met. Fever burned between them. Slowly, he urged her to let him in. Her body relaxed; his fingers slid in.

"Hmm," he moaned. So wet for him.

Gently, he grazed over the sensitive spot, she tilting forward deliciously, eager for more pressure from his hand. He was only too willing to oblige. Then, totally surprising him, she reached out and ran her timid fingers along his erection as though glossing over silk. She was driving him insane.

He slid his fingers against her and she clamped her warm hand over his shaft nice and tight, nibbling at his ear, kissing his temple and the blade of his jaw.

Her hand stopped moving. She was on the brink. Her thighs gripped around his hand, her muscles clenched, her buttocks raised above the bedroll and her breasts peaked toward the sky.

With a sweet moan, her body shuddered, her muscles squeezing and releasing. He'd found more pleasure in watching her climax than he'd thought possible, this beautiful woman who was sharing his ground.

But instead of subsiding, Autumn found his erection, stroking one side and then the other, then curling her fingertip around the top, making him groan with raw abandon.

"You'll spook the horses," she whispered.

He turned an eye toward her and noticed the faint smile. Teasing him, testing him, waiting to see how much he wanted and maybe how much control he had.

None. Dammit, none.

She continued stroking him, rolling him over to the side, her breasts flopping against his ribs, skin-to-skin and heartbeat-to-heartbeat. The gentle tips of her areolae, those luscious plums, grazed his flesh and made his body strain in sweet agony.

He came in that position, on the towel on her belly, disbelieving he was with this beautiful wench, this woman who'd had the strength to stand up to him and his men, this delicate vixen who was so soft in places he could barely recall.

It was roughly ten minutes later when they moved.

Watching her bare breasts move up and down with her breathing, Quinn was hypnotized. Those round perky tips, the little bumps along the borders of her areolae responding to the wind. She slid her blouse over her breasts. Gently, he tapped her rump. She buried her face in the blanket he'd rolled up to use as a pillow. Almost shy, she peeked out with one dark eye.

"The fire's almost out," she said.

"Hey. Don't avoid the subject."

"What subject? We weren't talking."

"You and me. And what just happened."

"What did just happen?" she asked, the expression on her face unwilling to let him in, shielding herself from whatever she was truly feeling.

"Well, let's see. You had your hand on my—"

She slapped his shoulder. "Shh."

"The horses can't understand English."

She turned to face the purplish sky. Did she feel as trapped as the midnight sun, caught half in day, half in night?

He'd been with many women, but he'd never done *that*. They'd been solely and completely aroused by each other's touch alone.

Some would call it sex, plain and simple. But it was much more complex, deeper on many levels. He'd had sex many times, and *that* wasn't *this*.

"What we did was wrong," she whispered into her blanket.

Regrets. They always came, didn't they? With decent women, anyhow. Not just on their side of things, but on his, as well. He ran a hand along her sleeve but she didn't respond.

"Hungry?" he asked, trying to think of something to put her back at ease.

"No. I'll…I'll eat in the morning." She got up on a knee. "I should move over to my—"

"Stay where it's warm. I'll take the other bedroll."

She eased herself back onto his blankets. "All right. Thank you."

Class dismissed.

Of course she'd dismiss him. She had every right to. She was a lady who likely imagined a future with someone upstanding. He saw the turmoil etched in her face. And he was someone she'd barely met. A man who'd wrenched her from her friends to steal her away in the middle of the night.

But as he heaved himself onto the icy blanket on the other side of the fire, he knew, too, that although they were strangers, what they'd shared tonight had been incredibly personal.

Autumn couldn't sleep. One would think the relaxed state of her muscles would immediately capsize her into slumber, but it was her mind that kept unreeling like a fishing spool.

The lump in her throat had been building for hours. What would her friends think of her? She squeezed her eyes shut. More important, what did she think of herself?

That her attraction to this wanted man—an attraction she could no longer deny—had been her undoing. Had she no sense of propriety? No knowledge of right from wrong? Her thinking had been…just this one kiss, then just another, then just one touch, and pretty soon she'd had her blasted skirts up around her throat.

Blazes.

She didn't want to be that kind of woman. And yet here she was. Naked at the fire.

She wasn't some naive young girl of sixteen. She was a grown woman who'd traveled on a ship to Alaska by herself, who worked in a hotel that brought in all kinds of men—and sometimes painted women.

Lord, did this mean she was now one of them?

No, no, she hadn't done it for money.

She'd done it for free.

She groaned and buried her face in the soft wool. *No one had to know.*

This was between her and Quinn. A man she barely knew, yet felt more connected to than men she'd known for years. What did this mean, and how could she overcome it?

Sleep finally found her in the cool hours of the morning. A blessed relief to bury her worries in blackness.

Chapter Nine

Autumn stirred to noises coming from the river. The heat of the sun beat against her eyelids, and in that lazy moment just before consciousness, she felt secure and warm, sleeping in a cocoon of blankets.

"Gary!" a woman called in shrill laughter. "Gary, get your socks!"

Springing up, Autumn opened her eyes. Logs in the fire had burned down to red embers. Quinn's bedroll was empty.

Quinn. How would she face Quinn?

Was he calling her? Had she heard voices?

She listened.

"Gary," called the young woman again, faint in the distance beyond the trees. "Breakfast!"

Fearful of who they were, Autumn rose to her feet. Still dressed in her wrinkled blouse and suede skirt, she tidied herself. She raked her fingers through her hair, sprinkled cold water from her canteen into her palm and ran it over her face. The iciness made her skin rush.

Quinn appeared from the direction of the river. Guns at his hips in an easy stride, not at all troubled by the voices. He'd investigated, obviously, and felt no danger.

"You all right?" he asked.

She nodded. "Friendly folks?"

"Gold miners heading home. Come say good morning."

She walked toward him but he made no move to head back to the river just yet. He waited till she reached him, then put a hand on her shoulder.

"I'll ask again. You all right?"

In the stream of morning sunshine, things looked better. Her eyes stung from lack of sleep, but looking up into Quinn's dark face, the unshaven cheeks, the dark hair without the hat, the gentle tug of understanding in his eyes, she believed he'd never speak of the night again unless she chose to. He wouldn't embarrass her, he wouldn't read anything more into it than what it was—an emotional outpouring between two strangers caught in a sentimental time together.

Thank goodness…thank goodness the night hadn't been consummated.

But still…something of unsettling depth had occurred between them.

He squeezed her upper arm. "Autumn?"

His voice was deep and sweet, and she almost cried from its tenderness. This man had no right to treat her like he had—first scaring the living hell out of her, the next moment trying to make love to her. And she had had no right to treat him the same way.

"Yeah, I'll be fine. A little confused about what happened. How I allowed myself to…" She looked down at the ground and kicked at the ferns.

"I take full responsibility," he said. "I do apologize for leading you…into something you might be regretting now."

The lump in her throat returned.

Turning, he angled his arm across her shoulders, and she enjoyed the weight of it as they walked toward their neighbors.

"Howdy," hollered a woman in her thirties, plump and pigtailed and eager to please. "Name's Savannah." She spoke with a beautiful drawl. From someplace south.

"Pleased to meet you. I'm Autumn."

The woman squinted at Quinn. "Jim's wife?"

Jim? Autumn turned to Quinn, who was eyeing her. Oh. *Jim.* "No, he's just helping me get back to Skagway."

Autumn stepped closer to their fire. Savannah was boiling socks on a grill above the logs, in a pan otherwise used in panning for gold. On another grill, she was using a second gold skillet to fry fish.

It was a common sight. Most stampeders who'd traveled to the Klondike in search of gold never found any. Consequently, their outfits and supplies were used for whatever was necessary.

"My husband Gary's got a few blisters from his

new boots. Don't want them to fester," she said, "so I've been boiling his socks."

"I have an ointment with me you might try," Autumn offered. "A salve." A paste too sticky to have applied to a huge wound like Harrison's. Besides, she'd left most of the medical bag's contents with Quinn's brother, should he need it.

"Heavens," Savannah cooed. "The Lord has heard my prayers."

Gary appeared from the riverbank. He was thinner than his wife, and perhaps a bit younger with a soft head of blond hair and wispy beard. He limped as he hauled two buckets of water.

Quinn rushed to his aid. "Let me help you."

"Rather do it myself, thanks. If I let you take one, I can't balance the other."

The man seemed capable, despite the sore feet.

The smell of frying fish made Autumn's stomach growl from hunger, but she declined the offer of food. "We've got plenty at our camp."

"Please stay a while. Join us for coffee."

"Sorry, we're in a hurry to get back," said Autumn.

The couple managed to stretch out the minutes anyway. Quinn and Autumn revealed as little as possible about themselves, but Savannah and Gary told their life history. From how they sold everything on their farm in Georgia to come to Alaska, to how Gary's rheumatism was acting up, to how they were packing their things and were now moving to the territory of Arizona.

Autumn and Quinn were just pulling away when the couple broke the more interesting news.

"I'll bring over that salve," Autumn was saying as she turned toward her camp.

"Much obliged," hollered Gary. "And if you're headin' any farther up, past Skagway to the mountains, watch out for that den of snakes!"

"Snakes?" Quinn turned to face the couple.

"No-good thievin' bunch of crooks. They attacked us in the mountains, but when they realized we didn't have any gold, they went after another couple right behind us. Slit their throats for twenty thousand dollars' worth of nuggets."

Autumn balked at the news.

"There's a bunch of them working together?" asked Quinn.

"Yes, sir. Must have a ring of twenty or twenty-five. Maybe more. Some of 'em pretend they're tax officials from the Canadian government. Others make you believe they're trained guides, willin' to help you along the trail."

"Thanks for the warning."

"Folks are wisin' up, though," said Gary. "They're banding together. The ones who've struck it really rich have hired guards of their own to navigate the mountain passes back to Skagway."

For some reason, Autumn noted, Quinn paled at this bit of news. His eyes flickered and he rubbed the side of his jaw.

Skagway was the major shipping route out of here,

thought Autumn. Anyone who'd found gold in the Klondike brought it back through Skagway. There were some land routes a man could take down through Canada, but she had heard they took a year or two on foot, and gold was too heavy to haul that way.

Gary had no more to add.

"Enjoy your meal," Savannah hollered as Quinn and Autumn made their way back through the tangle of trees.

Autumn turned to Quinn as soon as they were out of earshot. "What's wrong?"

"If folks are banding together, it's just what Brander's waiting for. One last, huge haul of gold he can steal before he blasts his way out of Alaska, back to the lower states and gone forever."

"That's just a guess on your part."

"Pretty good one."

The thought echoed through Autumn's mind as they ate and packed up. She thought of it again as she shared her liniment with Savannah, and when she slid into her saddle.

The other thing she was quite aware of, despite her intention to ignore it, was that the last time Quinn had touched her was two hours earlier when he'd looped his arm across her shoulders on the way to say howdy to their neighbors. She ached for contact.

By Autumn's silence and the occasional twisted expressions on her face while she was riding, Quinn was figuring she was awful sorry about their night together. He thought it'd been one hell of a charming evening, but her distance was like a bucket of ice between them.

When they arrived on the outskirts of Skagway three hours later, where log cabins began to appear beyond the thinning willow trees, she hollered for him to stop.

The path widened and she slowed her mare beside his. "If there was a way you could stay a few days in Skagway—to help you gauge the deputy marshal's next move—would you?"

Quinn lowered his head beneath a full branch of green shoots to avoid knocking his Stetson.

"Might help," he said. "Never had a chance to watch him up close. See how he runs the town."

"It would give an opportunity for a person to ask around."

"For you to ask around, Autumn? Verify my story? Is that what you're thinking?"

"No person in their right mind simply accepts what another person says about a third person, and should there be a fourth—"

"Hold on. Hold on. You're talking in circles."

"I don't know the deputy marshal that well, but I have had conversations with him. And I've known him longer than I have you. So, yes, you're right. *I* want to ask some questions."

His jaw tightened.

She still didn't entirely believe Quinn, but she was weighing the situation, and he should be pleased by that. In fact, he was very pleased, but dammit…they'd shared a night together and didn't that amount to some sort of trust?

Maybe it made things worse between them. He'd been trying for the last three hours to find a way to end things, to say so long and have a good life, and a safe journey home if you ever head back to Seattle, but the words hadn't come out.

She, too, wasn't mentioning any goodbyes.

He imagined there was a man waiting for her to return, was probably sitting on her porch this very minute, hat in hand, waiting to hug and kiss and celebrate when he saw her face again.

A flash of jealousy curled through Quinn.

He reminded himself to focus ahead. Exposing Brander for his cutthroat ways was both a business and personal matter for Quinn. How could his life go on in either direction without getting his face off those bloody Wanted posters?

Brander wouldn't recognize him. Not likely. They'd never met, and with his shave and cut, he looked a lot different from the poster. Autumn had recognized him, but that's because he'd told her who he was, and she was looking for signs of it in the poster.

"What was it that brought you to Alaska?" she asked.

"The hope of practicing law in a lawless district. And to help Harrison invest in some properties. He's the rancher in the family now."

"So you came to Alaska with money?"

He tilted his head. It wasn't like her to ask about finances. She must've realized how awkward it sounded, for she shooed the flies from her face and, flustered, gripped her saddle horn.

"Brander took it off my hands."

Her brown eyes rippled. "Ahh. And therein lies the connection."

So that's what she was after—how his relationship with Brander had started.

"The only connection I envision is my fist to his face."

She pulled in the corner of her mouth. "Would you be too hotheaded to stay in town, then? Could you handle seeing him up close, or would it tempt you to jump him before you're able to prove a thing?"

She had a way of wording things that cut straight to the heart of every conversation. Frank and direct, the way he and his brother talked to each other, but very few others. Certainly never a woman.

Quinn understood she was asking a valid question, and she deserved straight talk in return. "I could handle it."

"You could be my investor."

"How's that?"

"I'll say I found an investor and that's why I left—to chase my dream for a couple of days."

"Investor for what?"

"The Imperial Hotel."

He tapped his horse with his heels and spurred her onward, between the snow-covered mountains. So the lady had plans of her own. Mighty big ones, at that. He'd seen the famous Imperial from a distance. Had never stepped inside.

"Where would I stay?"

"At a hotel."

"Where do you live?"

"In a boardinghouse." Autumn paused for a moment. "You're supposed to meet your friends in a day or two. How will you get word to them you'll be delayed?"

"They'll know."

"How will they know?"

"When I don't show up, they'll know."

She opened her duster. In contrast to the frigid nights, the days were quite warm. Her movements revealed her pretty blouse.

"Why do you want to do this?" He tightened his hold on the reins. "Because of last night?"

She glanced away from his watchful gaze. To the river's edge and a flock of blackbirds settling into a pine tree.

"What happened last night," she explained, "let's pretend it didn't. I don't normally behave like that and don't know what it was that made me…"

Autumn pulled in a heavy breath, as though it was difficult to get her thoughts in order. "To make it very clear, what happened last night doesn't have the power to affect my judgment today. But meeting Savannah and Gary, and other things you've said about the deputy marshal, I have an opportunity to help set things straight. I don't think I could live with myself if I was too chicken to try."

His gut pulled with respect. She was a remarkable woman trying to do the right thing. Even so, he felt her rebuff on a personal level, and his pride was urging him to say he could do this on his own, without her help.

She tipped her hand to the sun. "What'll it be, Mr. Rowlan? This time, it's your turn to trust me."

Chapter Ten

Hiding in the shadows past the Red Onion Saloon, Autumn peered around the corner and watched her dear friend, Victoria, study each and every face as she strode down the crowded boardwalk of Skagway. Victoria passed the broad square windows of the Imperial Hotel, Ben's Ice Cream Parlor across the street, and made her way toward the jailhouse.

Autumn sank back into her boots with sympathy. Victoria looked exhausted, poor thing. Likely from worry.

Autumn's muscles tightened as she prepared to make her move. Victoria took the stairs right in front of Autumn and plopped onto the moist earth. Her skirts fanned out as she pivoted around the boardwalk and then nearly crashed into Autumn as she jumped out of the shadows.

"Pardon me." Victoria dipped away from Autumn in her long leather duster.

"Victoria," Autumn whispered.

Victoria looked up and gasped. "Ahh!"

"Shh."

"Good God!"

"Shh," Autumn repeated, worried she'd be found out before she was ready. "I saw you coming 'round the corner. We've got to get home."

"Lord. It is you. I was just going to check with the deputy marshal if he got word from the posse."

Victoria's eyes skimmed over Autumn's tangled hair, the ruffled blouse and the red suede skirt Autumn was still wearing from Saturday. The grime of travel felt heavy on her skin, but it was miraculous to set eyes on Victoria again.

When they hugged, her dear friend let out a small sob. She wiped the wetness from her cheeks with the back of her hand and couldn't seem to get any more words out.

"It's all right." Autumn gently tugged her friend by the elbow and veered away from the direction of the jailhouse. "Let's go home. I have some things to tell you."

Deputy Marshal Thor Brander struggled to control his rage, but the beads of sweat rolled down his neck. His shirt collar needed unbuttoning to relieve the bulge of his throat. His spurs jangled on the boardwalk. Floorboards shook beneath his mighty weight as he stomped into his office and confronted his deputy.

"Wittmann, what kind of orders are you passin' along?"

Gripping his cigar, Frank Wittmann, as broad as he was tall, stumbled out of his chair. The jail cells behind him were empty today, but not for lack of trying.

"Sir, I told 'em not to."

Brander lowered his voice. His heart knocked against his chest as he tried to simmer down. His heartburn and indigestion were acting up again. What was it these past couple of days? He fingered his chest but the pressure remained.

"Is all that goddamn killing necessary on the trail? It's gettin' harder and harder to cover it up."

"They weren't supposed to slit their throats."

"Those miners were travelin' with a team of Olympic rowers, for chrissake. A whole team of athletes!"

"They're nothin' but a bunch of weak-kneed Brits. Afraid to piss in the wind."

"But now they're boarded up at the Imperial Hotel. Some of 'em wanna take care of the men who did this to their friends."

"They've all got tickets on the next ship to Seattle."

Brander felt his heartbeat subside, the perspiration at his temples cool. "All of 'em?"

Wittmann nodded. "Gone tomorrow. Might be athletes, but they're scared. They jumped on the free tickets."

Brander kicked his banker's chair away from his desk. It rolled out and slammed into the wall. He dropped into it and pushed his way back to the hacked-up desk that had served him for the last two years.

Last summer, when the town's greatest crime-leader, Jefferson Smith—nicknamed Soapy—had been gunned down in the street, no one in town had pieced together that Brander was on his payroll.

Stupid. They were all stupid.

It wouldn't be much longer, thought Brander. No sirree. He was getting out of this hellhole before September, before the first licks of ice set in. Even the devil himself had left this place, it was so goddamn cold.

He had one more haul of gold to nab, and it was comin' around the mountain as he sat in this very chair. Twelve gold miners, setting it up nice and easy for him, their golden eggs waiting to be plucked like in one of those fairy tales.

Brander would be home in Portland by October, gold in every pocket, weighted down in all his trunks, and *she'd* be waiting for him. All dolled up in the pretty dresses he'd been sending. Deborah hadn't replied to any of his letters yet, but she would. Even the mail was goddamn slow in this hole. Everything was forced to come and go by ship.

Wittmann offered a cigar and Brander took it. He ran it beneath his nose, enjoying the pungent aroma.

"That's more like it." Brander kicked up his boots and angled the spurs so they didn't gouge the desk. "Any word of that singer?"

Wittmann shook his head. "Posse's not back yet."

"I'm not convinced there's been any foul play. These

things are usually very simple to figure out. I think she went off a-whorin' with someone she met at the dance."

Wittmann snickered. Then something much more serious crossed his expression. Sliding open his box of matches, he lit Brander's smoke. Next he pried a note out of his pocket. "Got something else to show you."

Brander took the yellowed paper and squinted at the words:

I'm coming after you, Brander. There's no place to hide.
Quinn Rowlan.

Brander's tongue went slick. "Where'd you get this?"

"It was left in a cabin along the river. About two or three days ago. Must've been right after the shoot-out with our boys. When his brother got stabbed."

Brander let loose a hearty laugh. "This note means his brother's been hurt bad." He sucked in a cloud of tobacco, closed his eyes and savored the way it went down his lungs. "Serves him right for killin' ours."

He held the note to the end of his cigar and, when it caught fire, tossed it into the slop bucket.

Heavy footsteps rattled up the boardwalk and through their front windows. Leroy Kendrick, another one of his deputies, burst inside, flapping his hat on his long legs and catching his breath.

"Miss Autumn MacNeil's been spotted in town."

Brander rose to his feet, all six-three of Viking

blood and heritage. His voice was deceptively calm. "Where's she at?"

"The Imperial."

"Victoria, please listen." Through a private door, Autumn slid into a spot by the cocktail bar in the crowded dining room of the Imperial Hotel, and pleaded with her friend. It was an hour and a half after she'd first surprised Victoria with her arrival. Victoria had been gravely concerned about her and had looked everywhere before Autumn had returned. In the boardinghouse they shared together, Autumn had quickly washed, combed her hair and changed. She felt more comfortable in her own clothes—a low-cut mauve blouse with its dozen pleats rolling down her bosom, and a black fitted skirt that hugged her hips.

"He's not that type of man," Autumn whispered. She picked up a red linen napkin from the stack beside the clean glasses and folded it, pretending to occupy herself with something useful. "I believe he's telling me the truth."

"He took you by force."

"Please," said Autumn, wishing her friend would lower her voice, "don't say anything to anyone until you meet him yourself." Autumn scanned the diners seated at the tables. No one had noticed her yet. "He'll be here any minute."

Autumn had confessed almost everything to her friend, whom she'd sworn to secrecy, but she hadn't shared the details about her tryst. The memory of Quinn naked still made her throat pound.

Victoria nudged her. "I just heard a rumor. I have to tell you—" But Victoria was pulled away by a man wanting whiskey.

Autumn looked up again and there *he* was.

Quinn was strolling in, decked out in a gray silk suit that played up the deep hue of his skin, a brown tie that matched the chestnut color of his hair and eyes and a white ruffled shirt that softened the severity of his sharp stare. He wasn't staring at *her,* though, Autumn realized with a disappointed pang. He was intent on reading the menu a waiter handed him as he was led to a solitary table. Quinn glanced up at the paintings on the wall, but not at her. Didn't he see her?

Acting nonchalant, Autumn peered up at the clock above the pine bar. One-thirty. Plenty of time still before she saw the banker. She'd made it home in time, she thought with relief.

Waiters in black tails and pressed shirts milled about the gilded room, hoisting trays filled with champagne glasses, lobster bisques and pickled beets fresh off the ships.

Breathless, Victoria returned to Autumn's side.

Autumn folded another napkin. "He's here."

Victoria looked up abruptly toward Quinn, then had the sense to focus back on their task. She groped for a napkin with trembling fingers. "For your own good, you must tell the deputy marshal. That man sitting over there is an *outlaw.*"

"I…I think I know what I'm doing."

"You *don't*. Let the law handle this."

"You know why I can't."

"*All* of them corrupted? Is that what you believe? This…this coward comes into your life, terrifies us all, you spend three days with him and you believe him?"

"It's not… You have to meet him, Victoria. He's got a brother he cares for. It's complicated."

"It's simple. He put his brother's value above yours."

It was that comment that made Autumn hesitate. The truth of her friend's words stung. He *had* put Harrison above the safety of a woman he'd believed was a nurse. He hadn't truly cared how frightened she would be, how traumatized and disbelieving.

Victoria nudged her. "What was it you said your grandma used to tell you?"

Autumn studied Quinn's easy expression as he read from the menu, as carefree as one could ever imagine. He glanced up again at a mirrored wall hanging across from his table.

She recalled her grandma's words. "Be careful because not all bad men are ugly."

"*Exactly.*" Victoria sniffed and craned her head over her shoulder to take another gander at Quinn. "That's what makes this one so dangerous."

Thoughts of her grandmother loomed in Autumn's mind. She'd been such a patient woman all her life, until the end when there was no one else to turn to, no one else who could help a sickly old lady and a young granddaughter who may have had the singing voice of a nightingale, some had said, but whose best option was to marry someone of stature to sustain them both. Autumn felt a tide of shame for how close she'd come to that endeavor, and how far she'd been willing to go to save herself from the streets.

Grandma wouldn't have trusted Quinn. She would urge Autumn to listen to her friend.

"Oh, Saints of Columbus!" Coming up from behind, her favorite waiter, Randall Yates, short and stocky with gray at his temples, slammed his tray on the bar and kissed Autumn on the cheek. "I can't believe you're here. I can't believe it. Where on earth have you been?"

"Out of town for a couple of days…"

He gripped her elbows and stared hard. "Are you all right?"

She nodded.

"Where were you?"

"With a friend…an investor…"

"Good Lord, girl! Victoria here was frantic. Cornelius couldn't sing last night, he was so upset. And I haven't slept a wink. Look. Look at these rings under my eyes."

He gave her another squeeze, while Autumn lowered her voice in hopes he would lower his. "I'm sorry I worried you all."

He kept booming. "The only one who wasn't affected was—"

"Randall," Autumn interrupted as heads began to

turn, "it's so good to see you." She helped him load his tray of bread rolls and butter, and he quickly pitched in.

"Thank you, thank you," he said. "I'm behind on table four, but when I catch up, you've got to tell me everything."

In his tuxedo tails, Randall tore off like a penguin who'd spotted a fish.

She glanced in the far corner and watched as Quinn lowered his menu to the table, lifted his shot of whiskey to his lips and glanced at the wall again. This time, Autumn's eyes strayed to his point of focus—the mirrored painting. She found his eyes there in the silvery glass, staring right back at her.

A quiver rolled straight down her spine. He'd been watching and noticing her this entire time.

Here, surrounded by the things she loved and the people she knew, he was on her home territory. Here, he was a stranger to her, an unknown man capable of unknown deeds. He even *looked* different, all polished up in a silk jacket he'd pulled out of nowhere, spiffed up like a presidential aide.

"Miss MacNeil," called a familiar voice.

In a flutter, Autumn glanced at the other doorway that led to the gambling hall.

Cornelius Castleman, the opera singer who'd befriended her from the minute she'd stepped inside these doors, wiped a handkerchief across his pale face. "Autumn. What are you doing here?" His normally rich baritone voice had a raspy edge.

He greeted her with a kiss to each cheek and held

her as if he'd never let go. It felt good to know how many folks had missed her.

"Cornelius, it's wonderful to see you," she answered. "I'll explain everything in a minute. I'm fine, I'm fine." She needed a moment to consider how she was going to handle Quinn. There was still time to turn him over to the law.

Luckily, an older couple beseeched Cornelius for an autograph, and Randall rushed over with his standard cup of tea for Cornelius.

"Have a seat," Randall told the baritone and proceeded to tell him what he knew about Autumn's disappearance. "Said she went out of town with an investor…."

The waiter led Cornelius across the room, to the opposite wall from Quinn.

She'd taken her eyes off Quinn. Blazes, was he still here? Desperation set in as she wheeled around to look at the dark mirror on the wall.

The galvanizing black eyes were still there, watching and waiting for her next move.

Lord, what should she do? There were so many people here, all friends, who'd stand behind her and protect her from this gunslinger.

"Who didn't miss me?" Autumn asked Victoria, a shudder creeping through her. "Randall said only one person didn't."

"That's what I'm trying to tell you." Fidgeting, Victoria dried the water spots from a clean champagne glass. "Mr. Kennedy."

"I looked for him earlier. To tell him that I'm back. The blackjack dealer said he was in a meeting."

Victoria groaned. "And while you were there, I heard a rumor. I can't believe it's true. Apparently, Kennedy—"

Suddenly in Autumn's periphery, a blurred figure came at her, and their conversation was interrupted. She looked up as this other man stalked into the dining room.

Deputy Marshal Brander. His tight expression was cemented on his face. Her stomach looped again.

This was too much, too soon. Her mouth went dry. She had planned to introduce Quinn Rowlan slowly. First to the hotel patrons and staff, then to the law. His meeting up with Brander was slated for days down the road.

Sunlight blasting from the high windows glinted off Brander's badge. Deputy U.S. Marshal. His guns weighted down on his hips, his spurs clinked with every stride, yet a warm grin settled across his face. It did nothing to ease her nerves.

"Miss MacNeil! Is it really you, or are you two up to more masquerade tricks?" Brander raised a thick brown eyebrow at Victoria.

Autumn felt a jab in her ribs from Victoria. "Tell him," Victoria urged through gritted teeth.

"No tricks," Autumn said to Brander, ignoring her friend's prodding. "It's me."

"A sight for sore eyes." Brander looked her up and down. "How are you? You hurt or anything?"

She nodded a bit too vehemently. Brander turned to Victoria, as if questioning the reply. Victoria nervously dropped a bundle of napkins, and nodded to confirm that Autumn was indeed okay.

Brander narrowed his eyes and drew his head back slightly, the auburn hair beneath his cowboy hat shifting over his ears. "Why don't you join me for lunch and tell me where you've been."

It wasn't a question, but an order.

Autumn swallowed, looked back to the dark mirror on the wall and met with Quinn's hardened expression. It was difficult to read him, for his face was dead serious, his lips unmoving, his heightened posture ready for anything…and guns beneath his suit jacket bulking up at his thighs.

She had to get out, and fast. "I've…I've already eaten." She lowered her sweaty hands and picked up her skirts, about to flee. "We were about to go for a stroll outside."

The deputy marshal grabbed her wrist with a powerful set of fingers. She'd never realized how huge the man was till she stood with her shoulder to his chest.

"Miss," he insisted. "I'd like you to sit down with me. Posse's still out and you've got some explaining to do."

Autumn looked down pointedly at the grip he had on her arm. He released her. "I'm here to help you, Miss MacNeil," he said gently. "Mean to do no harm."

It was his soft voice that lulled her. Her head spun with indecision. Trust him, or trust the penetrating dark eyes that watched and waited from across the room?

Chapter Eleven

He could take the bastard down right now. Quinn contemplated the idea as he sat at his table, watching Brander loop himself around Autumn. His men had sliced open Harrison's gut. One quick bullet through the heart, thought Quinn, and the world would be grateful.

But that wouldn't solve much. The reptile had an entire nest beneath him, other vile lizards doing his bidding, his stealing and his killing. Quinn planned on taking them all down. But first he had to lift the rocks off them to see where their slimy trails led.

And what of Autumn? Quinn watched her turn and hesitate toward him. She wouldn't cause a scene right now, would she? If she just calmed down, stopped twitching so much, no one would suspect she had something to hide.

Ah, hell, he thought, watching her run her hands

nervously up the back of her neck, then her bun. She hadn't changed her mind, had she?

She was in this with him. *With him.*

Coming back to Skagway had been her idea to begin with.

Quinn had watched her friend, the other lady, nattering at her in hushed whispers for twenty minutes. Dammit, maybe he should've left when he'd seen that. This town wasn't filled with folks ready to be friendly to a man whose picture was nailed up at the jailhouse.

Brander. A goddamn lawman.

Disgust crept up Quinn's throat.

This time, Quinn would get proof. Not just one man's word against another's. Proof.

With or without Autumn.

He watched her take a deep breath. She heaved her tight shoulders in that pretty little outfit she was wearing, pivoted on her heels and charged straight at him, with Brander in tow.

Quinn jerked forward. What now?

He slid to his feet to face them, nice and steady, parting his silk jacket so his guns were handy.

If it was killing Brander wanted, it was killing he'd get.

They reached him. Autumn's mouth trembled as she nodded hello to Quinn. The other one, the reptile, gave Quinn a cold glare. Brander's brown mustache flickered in the sunbeams that sliced through the windows. Quinn was surprised the man didn't turn green or something, the way lizards did.

"Mr. Jim Windsor." Autumn gulped down her words as she addressed Quinn by the phony name. "I'd like to introduce you to Deputy Marshal Brander."

Neither man removed his hat. Neither man made a move to shake.

"I believe we've met before," drawled Brander. "I've seen you someplace."

Autumn's eyes widened in panic.

"Have you?" Quinn gritted his teeth, so very aware that Brander's fingers were closer to his own guns than Quinn's.

"The masquerade ball." Brander's dark eyes seared through him.

"Right." Quinn relaxed his stance. "I recall noticing the man with the badge."

Brander patted the silver star pinned to his chest. Quinn wanted to kill him for what it stood for. Courage and trust from townsfolk this man spat on.

And twenty-six thousand dollars in a bank account meant to buy some nice property for Quinn and his brother. To start up a law practice, buy a horse or two, maybe even fund Harrison's desire to stake a claim in the Klondike. But Brander had ensured they never got to the gold fields.

"Now you're back," said Brander.

Quinn swallowed the bitter lump in his throat. His nostrils flared from the imaginary stench of the man standing across from him. Then Quinn bit down hard on his pride and extended his hand.

Brander shook it hard. In fact, neither man

seemed to want to be the first to let go, in an unspoken duel.

"Well," said Autumn, attempting to move things along. "The deputy marshal here was asking questions about Saturday night. I thought…I thought we might join you and…"

Quinn released his hand and gathered his wits. "Of course. Have a seat, please."

Both men went to hold out the chair for Autumn, but the reptile was closer, so Quinn let him win.

"Jim Windsor, huh?" Brander removed his hat and planted it on the wall hook by their table. Quinn did the same, out of respect for the lady.

Brander shoved his thick sausage fingers through his hair. "Never heard the name before."

"I've heard yours," Quinn answered. "Everyone around these parts knows what a closed fist you keep on crime."

Autumn's eyes flickered. Brander rubbed his mustache. "I try my best. I've got a few questions to ask the both of you."

"Go ahead," Quinn drawled. "Shoot."

Autumn kicked his foot under the table.

"Where'd you meet?"

"Mr. Windsor surprised me on Saturday eve—"

"No," Brander interrupted her. "I mean when did you *first* meet? Couldn't have been Saturday night. Not very many women would go off with a man for two days."

The lizard was smart.

"You're right," Autumn said quickly, her trembling fingers gripping the napkin on her lap. "He was in the audience a few weeks ago. You might recall the night of the big show, when that troupe from Chicago sang?"

Quinn didn't flinch. He'd go along with whatever she was saying.

Brander frowned. "Hmm."

The waiter slid by, pouring two cups of coffee for Autumn and Brander.

Brander stirred in a spoon of sugar. "I'll take the daily special." He turned to Autumn. "So tell me, Miss MacNeil, where exactly were you these last two days?"

Quinn was itching to jump in, but he'd follow her lead and fill in the gaps where necessary. He'd often observed in life that the less a man spoke, the more he had to say.

"Up the canal to Dyea."

Total opposite direction in which they'd actually gone, thought Quinn. And the town of Dyea was just as busy and freewheeling as Skagway, so Brander's men would have a difficult time verifying their whereabouts.

"Why?"

"Mr. Windsor and I were discussing an investment opportunity."

"Investor, are ya?" Brander eyed Quinn.

Quinn nodded.

Brander's shady eyes shone with greed. "What're you lookin' to buy?"

The corner of Quinn's mouth flicked upward. He couldn't control it. The son of a bitch wanted a part of everything, didn't he?

"Steamboats," Quinn lied. "Plenty of 'em."

He watched Brander's eyes glisten like two black marbles.

The waiter brought in a platter of breaded fish for Quinn, and crab for Brander.

"I've already eaten. Go ahead," said Autumn.

It was difficult to stomach eating at the same table as the lizard, but for the sake of his cover, Quinn dug in.

Brander cracked and sucked and ripped at the crab.

"Is…is the posse back yet?" Autumn asked him.

"Nope."

"I'm so sorry.… Is there any way to call them back?"

Brander smirked. "Shall I send out a second posse to look for the first?" He wiped his greasy fingers on his napkin. "Waste of men."

"Who…who went out to look for me?"

"You got a lotta friends, I'll give ya that. Two of the miners. Couple other regulars of the hotel. And Gilbert Oakley."

Autumn winced. Obviously, thought Quinn, she knew the Gilbert fellow. A jolt of jealousy hit Quinn, then a flash of guilt for feeling it. He had no right to be envious of any of her friends. She was a damn prize.

Brander smacked through his meal and addressed Quinn. "Steamboats are mighty expensive. And a far cry from investing in this hotel, as Miss MacNeil would like to do."

Autumn narrowed her gaze on the deputy marshal. She seemed to take great pains to control herself from blurting something out. Sipping her coffee, she set the cup down on its saucer with a loud ping.

Then finally, she spoke in a strained voice. Her shoulders were sharp points. "How do you know I want to invest in this hotel?"

"I'm the law. People tell me things. Safer for everyone that way."

Autumn remained rigid on her chair.

"I guess you're not too happy with the way things turned out, then," said Brander. "With Kennedy."

What did he mean? Quinn looked from one to the other. Autumn shuffled her feet and rubbed her neck. Her mauve pleats fanned out around her bosom. Brander noticed her feminine movements, too. Quinn's jaw tensed.

Whatever the comment meant, he and Autumn were in silent agreement to pretend like they knew. Autumn nodded solemnly, and Quinn finished up his meal.

"Waiter," he called. "Bill, please." He turned to Brander. "That is, unless you've got any other questions?"

Brander stared him down. This time, Quinn won because the other man flinched.

"Let me know if you need any advice on the steamboats. I know a few people who'll watch out for your interests."

I'll bet, Quinn thought to himself. "Sure thing. I could use the assistance."

At this moment, studying the sly glint in Brander's gaze, Quinn knew in his gut this was the way he would nail the bastard. Steamboats and investments. All he had to do was lay a few traps.

The waiter returned with the bill in hand. "No need to pay for the deputy marshal," he told Quinn. "Always eats free. He and his men."

The richest man this side of the ocean, filthy stinking rich from his crimes, and he never paid for his own coffee?

Quinn tossed a couple of coins to the table, rose and turned to Autumn. "Shall we?"

She got to her feet, tucked in her chair and nodded goodbye to Brander. Slipping behind the bar, she removed a beaded purse and large straw hat, then followed Quinn out the door and into the lobby.

"Where to?" Her neck was flushed with the excitement of escaping Brander. Her lips tilted upward.

"To see this man, Kennedy. We have to play along and pretend we're interested in investing in his hotel together."

"Wait a minute. I think it's time you met my friend."

"Who?"

Autumn bobbed around his bicep and motioned into the bar for someone to come out and join them. "The real Victoria Windhaven."

Quinn braced himself for the heavy pang of guilt

that set in. Kidnapping women wasn't his normal method of doing things, and he knew this Victoria didn't like him.

Autumn was still shaking from relief at their escape from Brander's clutches when Victoria stepped uneasily into the hotel lobby to join them. Wallpaper coated the high arched walls. A curved pine stairwell glistened in the afternoon sunshine that was pouring from the ceiling windows.

Autumn's high-heeled boots sank into the plush oval carpet.

In contrast to Autumn's exuberance, Victoria crossed her arms, shawl tucked beneath her elbows, and looked disapprovingly at Quinn.

"Pleased to meet you," he said, holding out his hand.

She needed a good jolt from Autumn to accept the handshake. "Am I supposed to be grateful that you abducted her instead of me?"

Quinn sighed. "She told you."

"Everything," said Victoria. "And I'll have you know I'm still inclined to go to the law."

Quinn swallowed. "That's what I'd expect from a good friend."

Victoria stood resolute.

"But if she told you *everything*—" Quinn turned to Autumn and she felt the smacking heat of a blush, thinking of their night together "—then you know what *Brander's* up to on the trail. Being a woman of medicine, I imagine you've got a heart for things like that."

Victoria frowned in confusion. He had a point, thought Autumn.

"If you prefer to tell Brander who I am, right here and now, there's nothing I can do to stop you. But your friend here has spent a good deal of time with me and she, apparently, thinks there's some truth to what I say."

He wasn't making it any easier for Victoria to dislike him. She rocked on her heels and with an exclamation of frustration, led the two of them out the doors for a quieter conversation.

"Did you get anything out of Brander?" Victoria asked Autumn. "Any comment…any proof that he's hiding behind his badge?"

"Not exactly." Autumn had hoped for something solid, some spoken hint that he was wrong and Quinn was right.

Victoria scowled. "See." Then, tilting her face past Autumn's shoulder, Victoria's mouth dropped. "Oh, no. Here they come."

"Who?" In a new bout of nerves, Autumn pivoted to look. Across the street, two men she didn't recognize walked down the boardwalk and entered the Imperial Hotel. One was an older gent in denim overalls with dark black spectacles, the other a younger man who limped and carried a cane. The younger one was dressed in purple pants, wore a sombrero and his blond hair was bleached almost white by the sun.

"Who are they?" Autumn turned to Victoria as the men disappeared into the hotel.

Victoria lowered her lashes, struggling to answer.

"You know them," said Autumn. "What is it? Why'd they go into the hotel?"

"To meet Kennedy."

Autumn's frustration mounted. "Why is everyone talking about Mr. Kennedy?"

Victoria tapped her boots in the cracked dirt of the street. She looked to Quinn, scrutinizing his face and his clothes. "It's what I've been trying to tell you. Kennedy never spent one moment worried about you, Autumn. Cornelius told me he didn't raise an eyebrow when you didn't show up to sing last night."

"But a posse went out," said Autumn. "He wasn't concerned?"

"Thought you were up to some trick."

Quinn remained focused. "Who are those men, Miss Windhaven?"

"I believe the new owners of the Imperial Hotel."

There was a stunned silence as Autumn tried to understand. She stumbled backward and gripped tight to the boardwalk railing. "What?" she breathed, shocked to her boots. "That can't be."

"Rumor is he sold it this morning."

"But I've got more than an hour left before I meet with the banker. Kennedy said he'd give me a chance to come up with the money. He *promised*."

"You know Kennedy," Victoria said with disdain.

With a shove past her friends, Autumn charged at the hotel, skirts flying, nostrils flaring, heading straight for her employer and the smug grin that surely adorned his face.

* * *

"Mr. Kennedy, a word please!"

Kennedy was standing inside with the new hotel owners as Autumn marched past the front desk and the bewildered clerk. The clerk was a young man who'd only arrived in Alaska last month and everything made him jump—from the sound of the bell when someone pressed it, to the hollering of the winners in the gambling hall when the roulette wheel landed on the right number.

Kennedy had one hand pressed to the back of the old gent in overalls, his other on the younger man's shoulder. Kennedy wheeled around at her shouts. When he saw her, he corked his face in displeasure.

"Miss MacNeil. Nice of you to show up. Maybe this evening, you'll find the time to grace us with your singing voice."

With a stiff smile pasted on his clean-shaven face, he turned to continue toward the gambling hall.

"Just a minute!" she ordered.

Kennedy dragged his feet, but the men turned around again. The older gent was getting nervous, fingers poking at his spectacles, the younger one removing his sombrero as she strode closer.

She eased up to Kennedy's big frame. "You sold the place?"

"Yes, ma'am. I'd like to introduce you to your new bosses. Effective tonight at midnight. Mr. Otis Forrestor and his son, Charlie."

Charlie held out his hand. "Folks 'round here call me Champagne Charlie."

The name sounded vaguely familiar. Ah, right. He was a well-known businessman in these parts. Had made a fortune hauling luxuries from the ships of Alaska over the mountains into the rich gold fields. In fact, she'd heard Charlie struck his first million selling imported bathtubs and champagne. The rich apparently like to soak in the bubbly stuff.

Flustered, she told herself not to take out her anger at Kennedy on these men. "I don't mean to be rude, sir," she said to Charlie, "but there are things I need to discuss with Mr. Kennedy. Business matters."

"Nothin' to say, far as I'm concerned," muttered Kennedy.

"You knew I had a meeting with the credit and loan manager. You knew I planned on buying this hotel. Yet you—"

"Shush," Kennedy said, brushing his hand in the air as though she were a child. "Not now."

Autumn colored at the rebuke.

Charlie hauled his shoulders back, taking a long hard look at her, then turned his somber gaze to Kennedy. "That true?"

"Mindless chatter of a woman."

Charlie looked to his father, then back at her.

"Well, then," Charlie said to Kennedy. "Seems you got yourself a problem."

Kennedy sputtered, then found his voice. "Now just a minute, here," he grumbled to Autumn. "You take yourself home and rest up for the show tonight, or I'll—"

"Or you'll what?" Quinn came up unexpectedly from behind and joined the fray.

Kennedy rubbed his lips. "And you are?"

"Someone looking out for her business investments. Jim Windsor."

Quinn made a point to shake all three gentlemen's hands. His presence infused her with confidence. "Mighty fine place you got here," he told Kennedy.

Kennedy wasn't amused. He rumpled the brim of his bowler hat. "Mr. Windsor," he muttered, "I suggest you tell her to step away."

It was the old gent's turn to intercede. "I don't rightly know what's goin' on around here, Mr. Kennedy, but I'm a tad concerned."

Kennedy's temples infused with color. "No need to be. No need to be. Why don't you two gentlemen wait for me in the gambling hall?"

With a grumble, Champagne Charlie and his father turned and headed down the aisle. Kennedy whipped back at her and pointed a thick finger at her chest. "You have no right to insert yourself in this manner."

"She has every right." Quinn's eyes flashed. His jaw stiffened.

"You left me stranded without a singer last night," Kennedy accused her. "You've got the whole hotel in a tizzy for where you've been. Hell, the whole town. Then you waltz back in like nothing happened and demand answers from *me?*"

"I can explain." Quinn stepped in. "It's my fault."

"I don't care whose fault it is." Kennedy bellowed, "Miss MacNeil, you're fired."

Autumn's heart hit the floor.

With that, Kennedy left the two stunned "business partners" staring after him as he pressed on into the gambling hall.

Chapter Twelve

Quinn couldn't believe what had just happened. "Autumn, I'm sorry."

"He was waiting to do that." She lowered her head and fidgeted with her fingers. "He was waiting for the first opportunity."

Quinn felt as though he deserved a lashing. He'd forced her to go with him on Saturday night, not caring what business she might have herself or how it might affect her private life. "I've ruined everything for you. I'm sorry."

The front-desk clerk was staring at them. Heads peered out from the dining room into the hallway. And Autumn's friend Victoria stood waiting at the front door. Judging by her fallen face and puckered mouth, she'd heard it all, too.

"Oh, Autumn…" Victoria gave her a quick hug as they made their way outdoors. "Mr. Kennedy is an obnoxious pig."

"I'll get another job." Autumn rubbed her cheek. "Something better."

Victoria tilted her head with compassion, but her look to Quinn indicated they all knew this was the best hotel in town. Everything else was much smaller, with not as big a need for entertainment. Some dance halls were downright dangerous with the type of men who frequented them.

Boardinghouses weren't cheap here, either, Quinn realized, so she had a hefty rent to pay. There was such a scarcity of everything in this town, prices were high. Not to mention the gouging that took place because everyone wanted a portion of the riches.

"Let's get you home," he said, wanting to comfort her. "Come on, I'll walk you."

"No." Autumn scratched her forehead. "I've got to think this through."

Quinn took a deep breath. He lifted his small sack of gold nuggets out of his pocket. "I'd like you to take this."

"No, I—"

"Please, I want you to have it. It would make me feel better."

She held the suede sack and squinted in the sunshine. Victoria stared, too, both women searching for something to say.

"I've been an awful influence."

"Mr. Kennedy was looking for an excuse to fire me. He never liked the idea that a woman wanted to buy the place off him."

"But he wouldn't have fired you now."

"Who's to say—"

"Autumn," Quinn insisted, "I think it's best if I continue my journey alone."

"What do you mean? You're leaving?"

"No...I think I'll stay a while." He nodded toward the red awning of the Skagway Arms Hotel, a quaint plank building half the size of the Imperial that sat at the crossroads leading to the docks, on Broadway Street. "I'll kick around for some information about Brander. But alone." He stroked her soft face. "You're really somethin'. Bye, darlin'."

"Don't go," she called.

He swung back around. "I'm doing you more harm than good. Goodbye, Autumn. Miss Windhaven."

Every step away from her was harder to take, but he tucked his hat on his head and kept walking toward the Skagway Arms. It was a bone-deep ache, knowing he'd never see her again. But *his* problems weren't *her* problems.

He had his brother to think of, Brander to outwit and a score to settle. The sight of one pretty woman was just getting in the way.

He was crossing the street to his hotel when the ladies caught up to him.

"Mr. Windsor!" Autumn called.

He closed his eyes at the sound of her voice.

She was panting when she reached him. Her friend, the nurse, could barely keep up. Both women plopped themselves square in front of him, beneath the red awning and the hotel café that was scattered with midafternoon diners peering through dusty window panes.

"Mr. Windsor," Autumn repeated, smiling up at him. The mauve pleats at her bosom shifted. Light caught the strands of hair pinned at her neck. "I do believe you're mistaken."

"About what?"

"What's best for us."

He peered to her friend.

Dressed more conservatively in a dark blouse, Victoria humbly extended her hand. "I think I misjudged you."

He shook the slim hand.

"You've obviously got…not only Autumn's best interests at heart, but maybe the interests of this whole town."

"Thank you for saying so. But I don't want to cause any more prob—"

"You won't," said Autumn.

"We'd both like to help," said Victoria. "With your cause." She looked pointedly to the jailhouse where the deputy marshal headquartered.

Quinn smiled. His grin stretched so wide, he had to take a minute to say what was on his mind. "You ladies do know how to surprise a fellow."

How could he refuse their help to nab Brander? For a year and a half, Quinn hadn't had one contact in town he could trust, and now he had two who were offering their services.

"If you'll excuse me, I do have to run," said Victoria. "I have a dressing to change at the Mercantile. Poor Mr. Edwards broke his wrist. I also have to check on one expectant mother."

"Thank you," Quinn called after her, knowing how important her vote of confidence was. He turned to Autumn. "Will you be looking for work, then? More singing?"

She peered at the pocket watch pinned to her blouse. "First, I've got an appointment to keep with Mr. Dirkson."

"But the hotel's been sold."

"It's not the only one in town." The wind kicked up at her sleeves and tugged at the wisps of hair at her loosened knot. "And I don't want anyone to *ever* be able to fire me again. No matter what anyone throws at me, I *will* own something here."

Quinn smiled at her persistence. "Yes, I believe you will." He held out his elbow and she grasped it. "Shall we?"

It took Autumn longer than Quinn expected as he waited in the trees beyond the stone building of Skagway Credit and Loan. He'd been pacing back and forth for nearly an hour, watching the townsfolk mill about their chores. He was especially interested in the comings and goings at the jailhouse. He'd watched Brander stroll in, one deputy stroll out. Ten minutes later, a bearded man, grimy from the trail, slithered in, looking over his shoulder an awful lot.

The wind whistled through the willows around him. Sunshine heated his sleeve, and he peered to the harbor where three ships were unloading coal, crates and barrels.

He heard light footsteps behind him and so reeled back toward the building. Autumn was just coming out.

It didn't take much to recognize the answer had been no.

She shuffled her feet. Her eyes were cast downward, her beaded purse dangling from her fingers.

What could he say to her now?

They walked downhill toward the river. Nothing needed to be explained. He'd seen enough of how she'd been handled in this town to understand her disappointment.

"It's hard when it seems everyone's against you," he said softly.

"It sure feels that way."

"Hard to know where to turn. What to do next. You begin to question yourself and your own decisions. 'Maybe it's me,' you tell yourself. 'Maybe I'm the one who needs to change direction, not them.'"

They'd reached a large plank house, three stories high. A sawmill down the road, just off the river, could be heard buzzing and chopping, men's voices carrying across the harbor.

"My home." She pointed to the side door. "You talk like you've been through this before."

"I'm still going through it."

"How do you manage?"

"I think of my mother."

"Your mother?"

"She was accidentally gunned down in a brawl. I was a kid. The only one with her. A twist of fate, everyone said."

She gasped softly.

"My mother didn't have an opportunity to fight back. There wasn't anything I could do to help her. But I can fight back for all the people on the trail who're being gunned down by Brander."

She reached out and touched his hand, gently weaving her warm fingers over his. A powerful connection surged between them. Her honey face and soft cheeks captured the light. Her big straw hat flopped across her face, shadowing her eyes. But he saw comfort there. And perhaps an invitation.

Gripping her key, she pressed it into his palm.

"Come in for a cup of tea."

His breath snagged in his throat. He unlocked her door, allowed her to step inside first, then followed.

Shadows of light and dark streamed into the hallway. There was a parlor and sitting area and a small kitchen with a cast-iron stove and chopping block. Knickknacks, bolts of fabric and a collection of pretty hats lined the far shelves. A lithograph map of North America sat on the entry wall.

"Hello?" she called.

No answer. They were alone.

She twisted toward the side table, to a matchbox

sitting next to the lantern, but he kicked the door behind him and reached for her waist. Then he drew her close and pinned her to the wall and kissed her.

She satiated his senses. Tightened every muscle, filled every pore with want of Autumn.

They shifted their bodies together, pelvis to pelvis, he remembering the night at the fire when he'd held her naked, when she'd whispered his name, when he'd brought her to climax.

The kiss was urgent, full of her, mashing their lips together. He traced her upper lip with his tongue and, in surprise, she met his tongue with her own.

Groaning with pleasure, unable to restrict himself to the kiss, he wrapped his arms around her waist, loving the slenderness. Reaching around, he began to unbutton her blouse.

She resisted, but smiled and laughed into his mouth, tempting him with her body as she twisted away. "Quinn…Quinn…we can't. *I* can't…"

"No one is asking for promises," he murmured. "Just a touch…"

"You want *more*…."

"Is that a crime…? To want a beautiful woman…to share a touch in this lonely world?"

He moved his hand upward through the splaying of buttons, to tug one sleeve off her shoulder.

She was so stunning he had to stare.

Her corset was strapless, a rich mauve color that matched the color of her blouse. Lacy along the top of her bosom, barely constraining her breasts. It pushed her cleavage upward and he lowered his head to kiss the sweet valley.

He heard her murmur, then he pulled away one of his shoulders, bracing his other hand on the cool plaster wall behind her.

Staring into her eyes, those rich ovals of brown flicked with copper, he swallowed hard and restrained himself.

"No more, then? You wish no more?"

In his arms, Autumn struggled to balance her breathing. With his dark face pressed to hers, her mouth still throbbing from his kiss—as well as other parts of her—she was determined to resist.

"What does all this mean, Quinn?"

He knew what she was asking. She could tell by the glistening of his deep eyes. No promises, no commitments for the future, no talk of courting, at least not in the proper sense.

"It means we've found each other, doesn't it? For however long this lasts…isn't it worth it? Even if it's only for this moment…don't you feel the burn between us?"

Oh, indeed she did.

His power and charm were intoxicating. No man she'd ever met lived up to the danger—and safety— she felt when she was with him. What a draw. To feel these opposite emotions. The rawness of his person, the integrity of his sense of justice.

He trailed a finger along the rib cage of her corset,

testing her response, asking in effect for her to make the decision.

Even with this, she respected his sense of fairness.

With a moan, she pulled on his hand, planting it squarely at the side of her waist, indicating her decision.

He wasted no time. Sliding his hands farther along her back, he pressed in again, thigh to thigh, and she felt how much she'd aroused him.

Mouth leaning down on hers, he was gentler this time with his kiss, his lips featherlight on hers, grazing first her upper then her lower lip, then his warm breath at her earlobe.

His lips trailed her bare throat, sending shivers through her. Reaching up, she stroked the back of his neck.

She felt him tighten in response.

He brought one hand up to the stays of her corset, discovering quickly this one was tied at the side of her waist instead of down the middle.

When it was loosened, he drew down the lace cups and inhaled sharply at the sight of her exposed breasts.

She didn't follow the trail of his gaze along her body, but enjoyed the cool air of the room against her breasts. She wondered what he saw, whether he was pleased at how she looked. Whether she lived up to his expectations.

He uttered a soft exclamation, and she smiled at the fervor in his voice.

When he lowered his head to pull at her nipple

using only his mouth, the burn sizzled through her core. A heat, a desire, an ache to be as one with Quinn.

Surprising her, he swooped down, picked her up and took a few steps into the parlor.

The windows were opened, exposing the beautiful view of the mountains, and a winding stream in the meadows—the reason she and Victoria had settled on this house to rent.

"Not on the sofa," she whispered with slight fear. "Someone might see." She knew Victoria was out on her calls, but a neighbor could pass by the windows.

"Don't worry," he said gently.

He planted her on the plush carpet between the sofa and chairs. Made of sheepskins sewn together, it was the softest part of the room.

As soon as she was down, he rose above her with one knee planted beside each of her hipbones, and tugged on her sleeves.

Off came the blouse.

He tugged next on the button of her skirt.

Off came the skirt.

Petticoats. Stockings. Pantaloons.

She was allowing him to undress her. Good heavens, what type of woman was she? If nothing else, she couldn't allow this to go far…. She had nothing for contraception…let alone the bruising that her heart might take when Quinn left this town.

"You are a vision." Quinn's face was infused with lust, his voice a low rumble, his eyes soaking her in as though he'd never seen a naked woman.

"Have you been with very many women?" she asked.

"Some."

"I'm afraid if I give in…that's all you'll want of me."

It was shocking how fast and hard she was falling for Quinn. Every other man she'd ever courted seemed like a faraway dream, more boy than man.

"You are remarkably beautiful," he said, stroking her cheek. "But there's so much more to you."

He pushed away her doubts with a kiss, this one on the side of her hip.

He kissed down her thigh, her knee, down her calf to her foot and the tips of her toes.

No man had ever kissed her feet. It felt terribly intimate, as though she were exposing a part of herself that she'd never thought sexual. But with Quinn, every part of her was sexual. Every inch of flesh, every rib, every eyelash.

Was there no place he wouldn't go?

She slid her hands upward beneath his shirt, loving the smooth expanse of his belly and chest, and he laughed softly. Helping her with the buttons, he was soon out of his shirt, too.

She unbuckled his belt, he with a bemused look of surprise, then undid the snaps of his fly.

"Autumn!" called a female voice through the locked hallway door. The door rattled with her bang. "Autumn, I thought I saw you come in. Autumn?"

The heat left Autumn's face. Quinn rolled to the side of her and quickly covered her up with his shirt.

"Landlady," Autumn whispered. She rose on an elbow. Her hair fell in disarray on her shoulders. "Yes, Mrs. Sebastian. I'm here."

"Good. Afternoon tea is ready. I've put out some of those biscuits you like."

"Thank you. I'll…I may pass today."

"Not feeling well?"

"A little tired. I'm in the middle of a nap."

"I'm sorry. My apologies. Carry on!"

Her footsteps faded behind the door, but Autumn's heart continued to thud.

"You all right?" Quinn whispered, hand on her waist.

"I'm not sure." She sat up, still covering herself.

"She can't know about us," said Quinn. "Otherwise she wouldn't have knocked."

"You're right…but *I* know about us."

Mrs. Sebastian's voice and her banging had brought out the truth of this situation. Autumn was an unmarried woman carrying on with a man she barely knew.

He must have seen it in the look of her eyes, for he exhaled with a heavy sigh, brought her blouse to her hands, helped her slide her arm in it, then turned to the windows as she buttoned up. She'd don her corset after he left.

He dressed in silence, tugging on his shirt, buttoning the black pegs, looping his belt over those hips.

Holding out his hand like a gentleman, he helped her to her feet. She walked him to the door.

He looked sturdy and suntanned as he stood at her door. "It's not wrong, what we did. The timing's not right, but this isn't wrong. Tell me you felt it, too, Autumn MacNeil."

Her mouth went dry.

"Tell me," he insisted.

She smiled gently. "I felt it, too."

With a lingering smile, he kissed the base of her neck and then was gone.

Chapter Thirteen

Quinn strode to the window of his hotel room, boots thudding on planks, and peered outside. It was getting late, past dinnertime, and he was still thinking of *her*. Autumn.

He knew he couldn't have her.

Well, that wasn't completely true. He could have a fling with her, enjoy the few days, maybe weeks they were together, and then what?

Promise Autumn what? Women expected promises, they all did no matter how much they denied it. What if this thing with Brander was never resolved?

Quinn rubbed his jaw. What if his face and his name were etched on Wanted posters for the rest of his life? What could he do for his livelihood? Pan for gold and hope he hit some? He smacked the wall.

Would he slink off with her on the next ship out of here? Was that a promise? Hiding out in the States and hoping to God no one ever connected his face with the outlaw's?

He paced to the other side of the room, past the narrow bed and writing table. He could legally change his name.

That wouldn't work, either. As soon as he walked into a courthouse and faced a judge to do it, they'd look him up in their records and arrest him on the spot.

Sorry, Autumn, if you'll just bear with me a few years, you'll be able to show your face again.

She was such a public figure, exposed to the scrutiny of audiences, and he was the opposite— needing to hide his face for fear of recognition.

How could they make any kind of life for themselves?

He was jumping the gun, though, wasn't he? It was silly for him to jump to the conclusion of a future between them. She had never said that. She never said she wanted him at all. Oh, sure, maybe he wouldn't have to push her hard to get her into the sack.

Guilt ripped through him. She was so innocent to give him the benefit of good intentions. He craved her body. Wasn't that all?

No, he thought with a sigh. He craved *her.*

But for cripes' sake, he'd only known her for a matter of days. How could he feel as though he'd known her for years?

He rubbed the back of his neck and stopped at the corner table to splash water on his face, hoping it would clear his mind. Because he felt as though the minute he'd met her, there was an acute understanding between them, the way they looked at life, the way they interacted with folks around them.

Maybe, most of all, his feelings ran deep because she'd taken it upon herself to help him in this town. She'd stood up to her friend, Victoria, she'd stood up to Kennedy, she'd even looked Brander square in the eye.

What'd she get for her troubles? Fired.

A rap on the door took him out of his thoughts.

He opened it. A hotel clerk, a young man barely old enough to shave, handed him a folded note.

"What's this?"

"Didn't read it, sir."

The young man left and Quinn closed the door. He unfolded the creamy linen paper.

Dear Mr. Windsor,
I thought you'd be interested in joining me at my audition at the Winchester Roadhouse, eight o'clock this evening.
Cordially, Miss Autumn MacNeil.

Quinn looked up from the paper. What did the little lady have planned? She was like a mountain cat. No matter what ledge she was leaping from, she always landed on her feet.

An audition for a new job already. But as pleased as he was for her, he wasn't sure he wanted to attend. He wasn't sure he could handle the way his heart rolled around in his chest when he listened to her sing.

Autumn pushed back the heavy velvet curtains from behind the stage and watched the gathering crowd.

Quinn wasn't here. Was he coming?

Nervously, she tucked her hair behind her ears and wondered again if she should have pinned it into a loose knot. As it was, her hair bobbed around her shoulders, wavy from the moist air of the ocean. And perhaps she should've chosen another outfit. She'd chosen her more conservative one—a peach jumper and a white pleated blouse buttoned to her throat. The linen jumper cupped her breasts in an empire waistline, then its straps swooped up over her shoulders.

Calm down, she told herself. With the burning limelight sizzling and illuminating the entire front of the stage, and the kerosene lanterns swinging from above, her peach fabric would have a pretty sheen.

It'd been a while since she'd visited the Winchester Roadhouse, but now that she was here, she'd be delighted to work on this stage.

She would. Yes, she would.

The seating was about one-third the size of the Imperial, but so what? She'd work more nights if she could to make up for her decrease in pay. The curtains were ragged, but who looked at curtains?

The place had one other regular performer—an old magician who drank too much, unfortunately, for he always managed to display how his trick was being accomplished as he stumbled through it. But who came here to watch magicians?

People came for the singing and the—she cleared her throat—dancing. Heavens, the young girls were all lined up behind her on the stage, ready to do their outrageous kicks in the cancan, wearing less with their fishnet stockings than some women did while using the saunas up the hill.

Sing, Autumn told herself. That's all she had to do. Now if only the pianist would take his seat.

He did.

She listened behind the curtains as the owner of the roadhouse, Mr. Lionel Hawthorne—the man she had to impress tonight with her singing in order to get hired—climbed the stage to introduce her.

"A special treat for you gents tonight," he shouted above the ruckus.

Chairs stopped squeaking, voices lowered, whiskey glasses stopped clinking.

"A guest singer, most of you know. The sweetest singing voice and sweetest face this side of the glaciers. Miss Autumn MacNeil."

The thirty or so men whistled and applauded, making Autumn flush with the fever of it all, giving her a boost in confidence and telling her in unspoken ways that she needn't worry, folks in this town liked her.

She'd land this job, she'd pay her bills, she'd save every nickel she could and her account would grow till she could afford to buy a business of her own.

Her heels clicked on the wood floor as she walked

across the stage. She made herself comfortable on a stool beside the piano. The room was small, warm and intimate.

When the piano began and she found her voice, she forgot about the ragged curtains, the drunken magician and the number of seats in the audience.

She sang a ballad about Scotland, a song her grandma used to sing to her. The words and the sentiments about an emigrating young son and the folks he left behind as he struggled to leave the land for America and build a new life.

It seemed to touch the audience as much as it touched her. Lyrics about leaving home and family behind, as everyone here had done in order to come to Alaska.

On the last notes of the song, Quinn appeared in her view. He was walking toward the bar as though he'd just arrived, or perhaps was changing seats from where he'd been sitting.

The lights reflecting in the bar's mirror struck his face when he sat down. She closed her song, the audience roared and Quinn finally turned to face her.

It was written in his expression.

The song had moved him.

His eyes shone with emotion, he fingered his ale with his thumb and his tender gaze locked with hers.

"Thank you," she said to the crowd's cheering. She curtsied. "Thank you very much."

Brimming with pleasure, she left the stage and headed toward the bar, where Quinn and Mr. Hawthorne stood close by. The crowd rose to their feet as she walked past, and although distracted by their hollers, she witnessed a man in a bowler hat and gold cuff links slyly whisper something to Quinn. The man in the bowler hat quickly disappeared into darkness, and the side exit.

"Sing us another one, Miss MacNeil," an audience member hollered.

"The dancers are ready to entertain you," she replied. "But if you'd like me back another night, you can ask Mr. Hawthorne."

Calls came in. "More, Mr. Hawthorne!"

"Get her up there tomorrow night, too!"

"Hell, the whole week!"

Autumn was full of good cheer as she reached Quinn's side. The corners of his mouth lifted.

Mr. Hawthorne approached her from the other side as the murmurs simmered and the men settled in their seats to prepare for the next act. She noted the two waiters were being hounded for more drinks—a wonderful sign that she'd created some business for the owner.

She tapped Quinn on the sleeve of his suit. "Hello, Mr. Windsor."

He touched the brim of his hat in salute. "Miss MacNeil."

"Well, Miss MacNeil." Mr. Hawthorne puckered his lips, suddenly looking quite sober. "That was acceptable."

Autumn groaned at his tactics. She gathered he

was about to offer her a position with as low a paycheck as possible.

Before he could offer her anything, two familiar faces appeared behind him. The men from the hotel—Champagne Charlie and his father, Otis.

"Miss MacNeil." Charlie removed his sombrero and leaned his walking stick on the bar. "Fabulous song. You're remarkably talented."

"Thank you." She looked at Quinn for answers, but as he stood up to shake their hands, he seemed just as surprised as she did at their arrival. "What are you doing here?" she asked.

"Yeah," grumbled Hawthorne, as though threatened by their presence.

"We were invited."

"By whom?" said Hawthorne.

Otis thumbed the air from the direction they'd come. "Deputy Marshal Brander."

The lawman himself strode into view. Autumn's heart thundered as she tried not to panic. He wasn't here to accuse her of anything. He wasn't here to arrest Quinn. She summoned her poise and glanced to Quinn's galvanizing gaze that seemed to say *keep calm.* But as the dancers began, Brander touched her shoulder and her fear escalated.

"Have a seat, everyone, please," said the deputy marshal. He signaled for the bartender as Autumn's stomach churned with dread. What was everyone doing here?

They seated themselves in a quiet alcove, stools

around the corner of the bar. In the background, the cancan dancers were kicking their legs and shimmying their calves, to major hoots and hollers.

"I told these gentlemen you were out of a job," Brander said to her. "And that you're looking."

Her hands relaxed in her lap. That was it? He'd come for an act of graciousness? "Thank you, sir."

She looked across the tabletop to Quinn, who was frowning.

Mr. Hawthorne didn't take kindly to the intrusion. "She's here auditioning for me!"

"Is she finished?" Charlie asked him.

Hawthorne swallowed.

Autumn nodded yes to Charlie. He leaned back so the waiter could deliver their drinks. The men drank ale while Autumn stuck with tea.

"Have you signed a contract yet?" Charlie asked her.

"Now just a minute here," Hawthorne interjected. "You have no right to barge—"

"Haven't been offered anything," Autumn replied.

"We'd like to offer you a job, then." Charlie ran his fingers through his light blond hair and sank farther onto his stool, clearly not intimidated by Hawthorne's blustering. "Same billing as before."

Autumn smiled, but before she could respond, Hawthorne did.

"But I was gonna offer her one!"

Quinn raised his glass. "Why don't you both offer her something? Make it good, fellas, she's got other calls to make."

Hawthorne squirmed. Father and son sipped their ales, chewing on the suggestion. Autumn looked gleefully at Quinn. She could have kissed him.

"Five percent more than you were being paid before," said Charlie. "We had a chance to review your papers and feel you were being undercut."

"Make it ten," said Autumn.

"And a cut of the liquor sales," said Quinn.

She reeled to look at him. Lantern lighting flicked against the contours of his face. He was dead serious.

"Hold on," said Otis. "We ain't made of money. We came to do some business with the little lady and didn't expect—"

Charlie nudged his father. "We give a cut to the male singers. Cornelius gets one."

Otis rubbed his forehead. "That so?" When he tilted his head, his gray hair flopped over his ears. He adjusted his spectacles. "But she's a woman."

"Still brings in a good deal of business," Charlie replied.

"No," said Hawthorne. "I can't match that."

With pleasure, Autumn stuck her hand out to the Forrestors. "You've got yourselves a deal." She wouldn't be the owner, but her wages would be higher, so she'd be able to save toward something.

"Won't take effect till after Kennedy's gone. Midnight tonight. Same hours you had before."

"Will do." Autumn shook firmly.

"Gentlemen, please, I beseech you," said Hawthorne, as the father and son rose to leave. "If you go settin' those kinda standards for women, they'll all be wanting them."

Otis patted his overalls. One of his shoulders seemed to be smaller than the other. Wounded somewhere from past times. "You're on your own on that one," he said to Hawthorne. "Good luck to ya!"

They left.

Brander looked on in quiet speculation, settling his sights on Autumn. Then on to Quinn. The deputy marshal was brooding over something, and it made her edgy. This close to a monster. Yet the monster had just done her a huge favor.

Hard to believe he was such a rotten human being. Could Quinn be wrong?

"I…I better be going." Autumn collected her shawl, which she'd left behind the bar when she arrived.

Quinn rose quickly, too, a massive man standing beside her. "I'll walk you home."

"Might as well go, myself." Brander got up and Autumn darted a nervous glance to Quinn. What did the man want?

They soon found out as they strolled out of the hotel and headed the few blocks toward the mountains and her home. She wrapped her shawl tightly around her arms, and Brander dipped unexpectedly, clumsily trying to help her.

She groaned inwardly. By the look of interest in his eyes, she knew one thing he wanted. She sped up her pace to get away.

"Spoke to a captain I know," Brander told Quinn.

"He's still in the shipping business, but he buys and trades them now. He'd be interested in talking to you. Helpin' you choose a good investment."

So that was it. The man had his sights on Quinn's money.

"Mighty kind of you." Quinn played along.

"I can arrange a meeting tomorrow, if you like. Stefan Yuri. His schooner is across from the shipping office and he'll be ready at eight." Brander spoke with a restraint she hadn't witnessed before. "If that's not too early for you."

Quinn adjusted his hat. "I'll be there."

Brander nodded. "Fine."

"Mr. Brander," she said. "I…I'd like to thank you for bringing the Forrestors around this evening. I never imagined I'd be so happy to get fired. Look where it's brought me."

Brander's grin seemed genuine. What if she were wrong about this man? What if he was just?

She had to find out somehow.

"Remember…Deputy Gil Mason?" She stepped over a protruding stone and hoped he wouldn't see through her question. "The deputy who used to work for you? Now there's a man who enjoyed the hotel on his nights off. He used to plunk down in the front row center. Watched every performance."

Something slipped in Brander's eyes.

"Whereabouts is he now?" she asked.

Brander glanced away to the harbor and the steamship just coming in. Dozens of sailors on the docks caught the tossed ropes and heaved the ship into position.

"Don't rightly know," said Brander. "Said he had other things to pursue and left."

"So he went back to his home in Alabama?"

"Yes, ma'am. That's what he told me. Back to Alabama to see his ma."

Her heart sank. His comment convinced her. He was a lying, thieving crook.

The huge Viking tipped his hat good-night and when they reached the corner, he turned right instead of left with them.

She waved with feigned enthusiasm, although the sight of him made her sick.

"Thanks again," she hollered. "I truly do appreciate your generosity!"

Quinn touched her elbow and guided her across the main street. "What was that all about?"

"Gil wasn't from Alabama. He was from Tennessee. And his ma had just moved to Seattle. Gil told me because he knew I was from Seattle."

"There's your proof."

"You're meeting with the devil tomorrow morning," she warned Quinn. "Please watch yourself."

Things had just become a whole lot clearer. Brander was involved with the crimes, Quinn was in danger and her feelings for him far outweighed anything she could have predicted.

When he stopped at her door, he unlocked it for her but this time there was no kiss, no touch on the waist, no recognition—at least in public—that they were anything more to each other than business acquaintances.

"Night, Autumn."

"Night," she said as she stepped inside and latched the door with a cold scrape against wood.

"Find the man in the bowler hat," Brander growled at his deputy when he returned to the jailhouse. His temples pounded. "Five foot ten, about thirty. Chopped brown hair. Wears gold cuff links."

Sucking back on a cigar, Wittmann stumbled out of his chair. He righted his huge body. Sweat stains circled his shirt beneath his heavy arms. Although he was heavy, he was always nimble on his feet, usually the first deputy to arrive someplace. Only reason Brander kept him around.

"What do you want me to do to him?"

"Have him followed. Even if it's out of town."

"How long?"

"Whatever it takes to get me some news. A few weeks. Whatever."

"All right. I'll get someone on it."

The cool pang of distrust seeped up Brander's throat. There was something unsettling about Jim Windsor, some reserve the man had when he squared up a room. Brander rolled a gob of spit in his mouth. When he'd first arrived at the Winchester, he'd stood at the back door along with the Forrestors and watched the singer perform. He'd also observed the man in the bowler hat whisper something in Windsor's ear, then the hard look that resulted on his face. Was Windsor getting tips of his own about the best stock to buy in Alaska? Did he have connections to bankers? How much did he have in his accounts?

It was all too thrilling to take in. Another stupid, wealthy investor about to be checkmated.

Chapter Fourteen

Autumn opened her eyes in the early-morning light seeping around her checked curtains, and lay there in her bedroom thinking of Quinn. The past few days spent with him had been, in order: terrifying, mystifying and exhilarating. Not to mention exhausting. She'd placed her head on the pillow at ten-thirty last night and hadn't stirred till… She glanced at the mantel clock over the fireplace. Seven-fifteen.

Seven-fifteen. Oh, no. Quinn's meeting was at eight. She ripped the covers off her legs, lifted her soft nightgown over her head and then, stripped naked, rushed to the basin to wash her face.

Cold water stung her cheeks. She rubbed her eyes, toweled off, then sprinkled baking soda on her toothbrush and scrubbed.

She hoped Quinn wouldn't get to the docks ahead of her. She wanted to be there for her so-called business partner.

Finished with her teeth, she glanced at the oval mirror hanging on the wall. There were several other mirrors she'd bought last year from a couple who were moving back to Washington. The frames were pretty, Autumn had thought then, and she could resell them when she found the right opportunity.

The wall mirror reflected her nakedness as she brushed her hair. She'd gotten too much color on her face over the last couple of days, as well as her hands and elbows. Her torso was cream-colored, her breasts high and tipped in pink. The muscles of her belly flexed and her bosom bounced with every stroke.

Her legs were untouched by the sun—wiggling pink toes, muscled calves and long thighs. The dark blond hair at the apex of her legs glistened in the pouring sunshine, squeaky clean from her bath last night.

Standing there naked, she turned her thoughts to Quinn. And would he like what he saw, if he were standing here with her?

Trying to dismiss her thoughts, she reached for her brush from the washstand, pinned her hair frantically above her ears and then scoured her armoire for something to wear. No time to get into a corset. She donned a tight undershirt that would keep her breasts from bouncing too much, a chemise on top of that, then a dark brown silky blouse with billowing sleeves that highlighted the color in her cheeks. She stepped into a stiff linen skirt that ran straight from her waist to the floor, and slipped into a pair of patent leather ankle shoes that required no buttoning.

"I'm off, Victoria!" Autumn shouted to her sleeping friend.

Victoria mumbled from the next bedroom as Autumn sailed past her, past Autumn's collection of alarm clocks, past her grandpa's sole remaining lithograph hanging on the entry wall. She had been seven years old when he'd etched the plate, and he'd allowed her to smear the ink on the press before he'd printed the brilliant line drawing of North America. Such a wonderful time it had been.

She bounced out into warm sunshine. Her pocket watch read 7:44. She hurried, holding on to the brim of her large straw hat with its billowing organza ribbons.

Last night when Autumn had confided about her good fortune in getting rehired, Victoria had been overjoyed at the news. And again, surprised at Quinn's role in asking for a portion of liquor sales.

He was incredible, thought Autumn as she nodded to neighbors on the boardwalk.

If things went well for him here…would he stick around? Could they perhaps court in proper fashion?

The alternative was too awful to think about, that he would leave as soon as his business was over. Her mind was rushed by doubts. How could she seriously court a man whose first meeting had been an abduction?

She could find a more suitable man when she was ready for marriage. Lots of decent businessmen came through the doors of the Imperial Hotel to rent a room, dine or gamble—lawyers and judges, captains of ships and former governors. Then there was her dear friend Cornelius, who was constantly asking her to dinner. Gilbert, who was still out on the posse searching for her—God bless him, she thought with a sigh—and Shaun, who'd more than once mentioned how beneficial a wife would be in starting a second bakery.

She didn't need someone whose face was sketched on a Wanted poster.

She didn't need Quinn.

On her way to the water, she dashed into the Imperial Hotel to double-check the schedule at the front desk. When she saw her name penciled in to the week's rotation of entertainers, she nearly whooped. It was true. She was rehired.

Back on the boardwalk, her footsteps flew as she approached the docks. Then turmoil set in again.

Perhaps she should leave. Quinn was virtually a stranger, and perhaps she was putting herself and even Victoria in jeopardy. Playing with fire by taunting the deputy marshal.

Gulls squawked over the inlet. The sun blazed on her face. She tilted her straw hat lower to shield her eyes.

"Mornin', miss," called a sailor unloading crates of preserves.

"Can I help you?" asked another, peering at her from beneath a black beret.

"No, thank you."

Small clapboard buildings lined the docks, along with rows of log cabins and the never-ending tents that were sprawled an acre past that. All filled with folks trying to make a living, selling fish, compasses, shoes and even newspapers two months old.

Ships and boats of various sizes rocked on the waters.

She fumbled with her satchel, pulled out her pocket watch, which now read seven minutes after eight, then turned around to head home…and ran smack into Quinn.

"Morning. What are you doing here?" He frowned, and reinforced her feeling of exclusion. She didn't fit in with him. He was an unknown man in her town, someone who had problems with the law far greater than hers, someone who had his life to figure out and profession to reestablish. Someone who had no business making her feel as though the earth froze on its axis every time she looked into the piercing expression of his handsome face.

It was a dicey situation, thought Quinn, and she shouldn't be here. The breeze off the coast rippled around him.

He waited for her answer.

The brown eyes flashed the same color as her blouse. The wind plastered the silk to her bosom, and he responded with a yearning he was beginning to resent. He didn't want to thirst after any woman. Not till he was free to do so with his name respected in the eyes of the law, a name that meant something.

"I thought I'd join your meeting. Give a recommendation, as a private business client."

"You're too late."

"Pardon?"

"Mr. Windsor," called Captain Yuri from behind.

Autumn ducked her head around Quinn's shoulders, and with a sigh, he swung around to the man he'd just finished talking with.

Captain Stefan Yuri, dressed in navy shirt and pants, in his fifties with the physique of a thirty-year-old boxer, saluted Autumn playfully with two fingers.

"Howdy." A gust of wind knocked her hat off her head. She yelped. Quinn grabbed it in midair and planted it on her crown.

"Miss MacNeil," Quinn introduced, "meet Mr. Yuri."

"Pleased to make your acquaintance." His English was thick with a Russian accent, but his words were perfect.

"Studied in England," he'd told Quinn forty-five minutes earlier.

"You're the one with the lovely voice," said the captain.

"Thank you," she called.

Yuri leaned against the rail and addressed Quinn. "Forgot to mention. There's a new banker in town. I do a lot of dealings with him. Caleb Shackleford." The name was quite a mouthful for Yuri to get out. "Tell him I sent you. He'll give you a good deal."

"Thanks for all your assistance." Quinn gave him

a final wave goodbye then led Autumn down the docks. "I'll walk you home."

"What was that all about?" she whispered.

"A mining expedition." Quinn nodded to two fishermen and talked softly against her shoulder. "I was sent here for the man to pick my brain. See how much I could afford and where I was stashing it all."

Autumn frowned. She nodded to an old woman dressed in a checkered brown apron. "So...he's working with Brander?"

"No doubt about it. So is Shackleford, I'm sure."

"What'd you tell him?"

"Nothing. But I implied I was loaded to the gills."

Autumn stifled a smile. "You baited him."

"He's definitely hungry."

They walked in the sunshine, crossing from the docks to a big patch of fresh grass. Autumn tied the silk ribbons firmly beneath her chin, so the wind couldn't snatch her hat again. She looped her arm into his, and for a minute he could pretend they were a couple.

Passersby nodded, and Quinn and Autumn nodded back. Just like that. He was respectable because he was being seen with her.

His thoughts turned back to business. He was pleased how the meeting had gone. It confirmed his worst suspicions about Brander, and gave him two more names for his men to check out—Yuri and Shackleford.

Quinn pressed his fingers to the back of Autumn's

spine, enjoying the way she felt beneath his touch. Then he released his hold. No matter how distant and cool he tried to remain with her, he warmed up quickly whenever she waltzed into view.

That was the bloody problem. And now this.

She craned her neck up at him and must've seen his sly grin. "What is it?"

"Someone's missing a certain article of clothing."

She flushed, looked down quickly at her stiletto shoes. The pointed tips appeared alternately beneath her long skirts as she walked. He even liked to listen to the swish of fabrics as she moved.

"Did you do that special, for me? Forget to put something on?"

"No." She pulled away.

Yes, she did, he thought. *She most certainly did.*

A cold shoulder couldn't stop him.

He leaned in close to her ear. "What else did you forget to put on?"

Her mouth dropped open and she gasped.

God, she was beautiful to tease. She got all flushed. Her eyebrows shot up, her eyes focused sharply on his face and her lips were halfway between a look of outrage and a smile.

Yup, she was teasing him with her lack of clothing. And he didn't mind one bit.

They continued beneath a clump of spruce trees till they hit the boardwalk that led into the main part of town. The buzzing from the sawmill half a mile down the other road echoed against the mountains.

An eagle soared above the slope to their right, over the hillside forest.

He felt good.

She simmered and they fell into place, like a man and wife might on a morning stroll from the market.

Longing raced through him, for things that were out of his reach. How could he make them *within* his reach?

How could he make *her* within his reach?

"You all right?" she asked, her smooth face skewered on a shaft of sunlight that sliced past the brim of her hat.

"Yeah."

"Now what? How do you propose to keep Brander's interest, when they discover you're *not* loaded to the gills?" She did a double take. "Or are you?"

"No." He might have been at one time, he thought, trying to temper his anger. Not abundantly wealthy, but well-off. He'd lost it to Brander, and it made his blood boil. "Oh, he's still interested." Quinn's boots slapped against the dusty boardwalk. "He's put a tail on me."

With alarm, she darted a look past his shoulder.

"Some guy's been following me since last night. Don't look now—" he planted his large hand on her slender spine and redirected her focus "—but he's about two hundred yards behind us. Carrying a newspaper. Wearing a miner's hat."

Autumn stiffened, but she followed his advice and turned to look straight ahead.

"Ready to outrun him?" A sense of adventure filled him.

She studied him beneath her stiff stylish hat. She had a potent blend of sophistication. And the slight bounce of a woman without a corset.

His belly tightened with a primitive urge.

She glanced past his arm in the direction of the miner, and seemed to understand Quinn's meaning, for she flickered her lashes and pursed those gorgeous lips. "Sure."

He grasped her elbow as they neared a cross street. "Here we go."

They took the stairs, landed on the cracked sand, he steered her right and they leaped into Ben's Ice Cream Parlor.

The man behind the counter was filling the cooler with blocks of ice. He had slicked-back hair and wore a spotless white apron. "Howdy, folks. Come to try our brand-new flavor? Marmalade?"

"Some other time," said Quinn. "Just passing through."

They scooted out the back door and nearly got run over by a bicycle.

"Sorry!" called the old man, swerving.

"In here." Quinn led her across the street into the Klondike Outfitters.

The shelves were crammed with rucksacks, tents, picks, shovels, gold panning supplies and rubber boots that went up to the knees.

"Are you seekin' adventure?" The shop owner peered up from a map he was showing a customer.

"Tomorrow!" Quinn squeezed past the bins of nails at the back and slid out the door.

"Think we've lost him?" Autumn, her cheeks blazing with the rush of excitement, kept walking.

"Better make sure."

Quinn then took her through the bootmaker's shop, where a young sailor was getting measured, and through two saloons that were already packed with customers, despite the early-morning hour. Next they ventured into the room of a fortune-teller who was eager to offer her advice on the subject of children—to which Autumn's cheeks dimpled with surprise. Quinn quickly guided her out of there, to the livery stables, where a mule brayed at his Stetson.

And finally, a half a mile past where they'd first started, he steered her toward the last buildings nestled on the outskirts of town, built into a mountainside. The men's and women's saunas.

A Scandinavian woman ran them, he'd heard. They'd recommended her services to him at his hotel last night, saying she was an incredible masseuse and could put a bull to sleep with her fingers.

Autumn turned around, so she was walking backward beside him, searching the street from where they'd come. Her hand shot up to her throat and she screeched.

Quinn turned around and took a good look. She must've spotted the miner's hat between the clapboard buildings.

"It's not him." He reassured her, nonetheless slipping into the main office of Miss Flora's Saunas.

Behind the counter, Miss Flora peered up from her knitting. "Massage for two?"

In beaded dress and blond hair neatly curled into a bun, she reached for two keys. One marked for a gent, one marked for a lady.

"Land's sake, Miss Flora." Autumn stepped up to the ledge. "You know I always come alone."

"Sauna for one then?"

Autumn peered back toward the door, still a bit edgy. Then much to Quinn's surprise, she took the key.

Well, now, what was this?

"She thinks you're just walking me to the door." Autumn, laden with fluffy towels, balanced on the narrow flagstone path leading to the farthermost cabin on the mountainside. Pushing up on tiptoes, she peered above the log cabin beneath them on the hill to scrutinize the buildings along the boardwalk below, terrified she'd see the man tailing Quinn again. "We'll ditch our things and run from there."

"No need to run," said Quinn.

"Right. Walk then." She turned on the familiar corner that led to the back of the shack, darting beneath the bushes, grateful for their cover. "Walk, so we don't attract attention."

"No need to walk, either."

They reached the back door and, exasperated, she turned around to look up at him. "What are you talking about? You're being followed. Brander wants to know your comings and goings."

"The guy's not following us anymore. We lost him at the first turn. The ice cream parlor."

"The first turn?"

He grabbed the key from her fingers and unlocked the cabin.

"I saw him head off in the opposite direction. To the jeweler's."

She planted her hand on her hip. "Then what was that all about? The saloons and the fortune-teller and the stables? Why were we running?"

"You said you wanted to," he replied with a gentle tease.

Then with a mischievous glimmer, he jumped into the darkened cabin, leaving her to stare after him in disbelief.

"Where's the lantern?" he called from inside.

The only light pouring in was the light from the door. She stepped inside and closed the door with a snap. Total darkness now.

She tossed her load of towels onto the table she knew to be beside the door, and he grew suddenly still.

"Where are you, Autumn?"

She knew by his voice where he was, but didn't feel like disclosing her position since he was in such a playful mood.

When he swung around, his weight creaked on the boards.

"Ow!" The banging of a steel drum echoed between them. Apparently, he'd found the steam tank.

Crouching, she searched the wall boards by her

left ankle. There it was. She unlatched the familiar hook. He must've heard the swoosh of her skirts, for he lunged at her just as she was straightening.

She gasped a laugh.

In the blackness, he pressed her to the wall, his hands tucked loosely on hers. So very close. So very tempting. Then he yanked her hands well over her head, trapping her. She felt his warm breath on the top of her hair. The body heat between them. The tip of her breasts inches from his chest. She wondered how that chest would feel, pressed naked against hers.

"Looks like you won," she said softly.

"What's my prize?"

"This."

With a kick of her heel, she knocked out the back wall.

Sunlight streamed into the back quarter of the cabin, framing the most magnificent view of the stream below, the ridge of emerald forest and a herd of shaggy white mountain goats balancing on a precipice, high in the distance.

A flock of snow geese fluttered their wings as they swooped by the door.

Stepping back in silence to get the full scope, Autumn and Quinn took in the breathtaking wonder of nature from the privacy of their own cabin. They were safe from the world, she thought, but perhaps not safe from each other.

She looked timidly at Quinn as he stared out, a

man whose face was notched with pride, eyes lined with laughter, mouth firm with the resolute knowledge he belonged in this world, along with all of nature's gifts.

Her breath tugged inside the hollow of her throat.

And what a gift he was.

Chapter Fifteen

After a few moments of absorbing the view, Quinn turned to the lovely woman at his side. "I feel I should apologize."

"For making my heart jump at every turn?"

"No, that I enjoyed."

She flicked her hair behind her ear in a gesture of light amusement and he was bewitched by her pretty face and her silhouette against the back boards of the cabin.

"Do I really make your heart jump, Autumn?"

There was a flash of movement in her throat. "All the time."

This pleased him a great deal. To know he wasn't the only one afflicted.

"I apologize for complicating your life."

She didn't immediately respond. She took what he said and perhaps mulled it over, for she turned back to the outdoor scene and watched as, just above the wire fence, dozens of red-throated birds settled in the trees.

"It's true. You have complicated it. But perhaps you only pointed out the complications. They were there all along."

"You mean with Brander?"

"Yes."

"It would be simpler if I handle him on my own."

"Simpler for me, yes. But in the scheme of right and wrong, there's no question I have to help you."

He reached out, touched her shoulder and turned her around. The friction between them ran like a shock of lightning.

"Autumn, you are special."

Her lips tilted upward and he was so tempted.... So tempted to take this woman and *be* with her. To show her just how much he felt when he was around her, how much she filled him, how his ears and his eyes and his skin and even his tongue seemed to be aware of her. From the way her lashes caught the ripple of sun, the slight bump on her nose, the elegant turn of her ear and the beautifully formed upper lip.

"Do I complicate your life in any other way?"

Her eyes brimmed with so much feeling he clenched his throat.

"In every way you can think of." Her voice was a soft ocean wave. "You've made it richer. Deeper. More frightening and more safe."

Overwhelmed, he grappled between pulling her

into his arms and going out that door and leaving her in peace. "Remember that night on the trail?"

A flush ran up her neck and she nodded. The night they'd spent in each other's embrace.

"I keep thinking about…the way you looked," he said. "The way the moon fell across your legs…the way you filled my hand, and my heart, Autumn…"

Her chin quivered, her fists tightened into her skirt and she seemed to be trying to make peace with something she was fighting.

Yet *he* fought for equilibrium, too.

Daylight surrounded them. The hum of a thousand insects sounded like an orchestra. The call of a coyote or a wild dog howled somewhere in the misted trees.

"Would it be so bad?" he asked. "You and me?"

"Don't ask. It's not right."

"We're not married," he agreed with a slice of heavy guilt. "You're a single woman with a reputation to uphold. Miss Flora down there will be wondering why I haven't come back out."

"She's…she's busy this time of morning, washing towels and folding sheets."

"You've been here often."

"Two mornings a week, if I…" Her lonely whisper trailed off.

Behind her along the far wall, the rocks of the sauna sat inside a large metal drum, with a row of tiered benches behind it. The water cauldron—or steam tank—sat above a ground-out fireplace dug into the dirt below floor level, with coals that were still slightly burning from whomever had used the cabin this morning.

"Is this place entirely fenced in?"

She knew, didn't she, why he was asking? He wanted to know about their privacy. Did they have total seclusion, or didn't they?

"We were having a problem last year with Peeping Toms. Miss Flora had all the cabins fenced in to protect the women."

Total privacy. Hallelujah. Every male inch of him responded with pleasure.

"Who are we kidding? I want to be with you, and you want to be with me."

Her nostrils flared ever so gently as she inhaled. She rocked back on her high-heeled boots. Her silky blouse cupped the expanse of full breasts.

"There was a time after my grandpa passed away…and then my grandma… I wondered what to do with myself with the great big void they left behind. All that empty space in my life. I was with… I was with a man…."

Was she confessing? Did she think that would turn him away?

"I hope you found some comfort there."

It didn't seem to be the response she was expecting. She tilted her head. "You're a surprising man. You're astute, even with people you don't know."

"I know you." He wove his fingers into hers and tugged her forward so that their bodies were pressed together. He reveled in her warmth, her humanness, her femininity in the simple way she held her head.

"I know you're a woman searching for something more. I know you're loved by this town. And I know—" He gulped, realizing he had to say it before he never got the chance again. "I know I want to feel every part of you with every part of me."

"Oh, Quinn…"

She buried her lips into his neck. He shivered with the exquisite pleasure of her touch. He smelled her hair and her skin, and she was like an angel.

She kissed his jaw, a thousand different ways it seemed, but still not enough. He kissed her temple and her ear and anchored his lips at the soft side of her neck. He untangled her hair with his fingers, gripping the silky weight, sliding his palm along her nape and marveling at the feel of her hand along his waist. She tucked her fingers into his side.

"You drove me crazy from the second I set my eyes on you." He tried to temper the knocking of his heart and pounding through his body.

He wanted to throw her down on a pile of towels, rip off her clothes and enjoy every luscious turn of her body.

With a yank on her hand, he pulled her toward the fireplace. He tossed on two logs.

"Won't take long to ignite." He slipped the towels they'd brought onto the spotless plank floor. They were nestled inside the cabin with a clear view of the valley. "Come here and kiss me."

He saw such tenderness, mixed with the bliss of desire in her expression, he stared for a moment, then pulled her down onto the floor in his soft toweled bed.

Lying beneath him as the logs caught fire and crackled under the open water tank, Autumn raised her face to Quinn's clothed shoulder and kissed it. If she allowed herself to dream, and dream big, she imagined a life with him beyond the next week, and the next and the next.

Softly, he undid the buttons of her blouse, starting from the bottom and working his way up. He seemed so sure of himself, and she so unsure…not only of what this moment held for them, but also for how she would react to his full embrace, to making love with Quinn.

Trembling at the thought of being with him completely, she curled her fingers up beneath his shirt and ran them on his tight belly.

His stomach tightened under her touch. His lips fell open. "You're such a fine woman. I can't believe you'd bother to have me."

"Bother? That's not how I feel when I'm with you."

He groaned and pulled the blouse off her shoulders. Rather than remove her buttoned chemise, he traced a gentle finger round her areola above the cloth, avoiding her nipple, making gooseflesh rise on her arms. Her heart hammered beneath her ribs, trapped in the rapture.

She kissed his arm, the one he stroked her with, and he dutifully removed his shirt.

Lord, the layers of muscles were mesmerizing…his tanned chest with a fine matting of hair, the ripple of muscled cords at his belly, the flat wide expanse of male beauty. His biceps flexed as he ran his hand along her rib cage, squeezing her tight as if measuring how much of her he could grab with one hand.

"All of me," she whispered. "Take all of me."

He tugged at the buttons of her chemise, then, cracking the fabric wide open, revealed the creamy rounds of flesh. He restrained himself, catching his breath as his eyes poured over her breasts. Did he like what he saw? The pink pointed tips, the swell of flat areolae longing for contact, cleavage begging to be kissed.

He made her wait. Tracing his finger like a blade up along each bare rib, he watched her reaction. Surely he could see her heart pounding for escape, the throbbing of each beat closer to leaping out of her skin. Could he see the perspiration along her throat, the heaving of her chest with every breath, see the heaviness she felt in every limb?

The whisper of the trees outside mimicked the rushing through her ears. Suddenly she noticed the beads of dew at *his* temples, the mad beat of *his* pulse at the base of his tanned throat, the flinching of muscles in his jaw and his belly as he traced those wondrous little circles on her stomach.

Surprising her, he scooped a water bucket off the floor by the tanks and tossed it onto the rocks.

A sharp sizzle fried the air.

Laughter escaped the back of her throat even as the ensuing little cloud puffed in the air above them.

"Sit up," he beckoned.

When she did, he watched the bounce of her breasts, the way they cupped the air, perhaps the way she didn't shy away from his look.

He tugged at the rest of her clothing, helping her escape the pull of her skirt, the heaviness of her petticoats, the length of her knickers and he finally tugged on each stocking, rolling them off her feet. He tossed them recklessly in a pile of his own clothes, as she removed those for him.

Naked.

The two of them basked in the private display, in their private quarters. With one of the walls open to the richness of nature, greenery to beyond the visual eye, blue skies stretched beyond the icy mountains with shredded clouds, she felt as though they were on a stage. Except they were the only audience, one to each other.

Moisture clung to her hair, enveloped her with warmth, made her feel comfortable and lazy and yearning to be stroked. He started at her feet, kissing the top ridge, then her ankle, her calf, the side of her knee, the crease where her thigh met with her hips. He was devouring her an inch at a time, lathering hot, wet kisses on her body in the most daring of places. From her hip, he moved to the inside of her thigh, up to her belly button, the side of her waist, up toward her armpit, jumping to her shoulder, her neck, her ear.

"Kiss me on the mouth," she begged, wrapping her arms up over this gorgeous statue of a man, who was as firm as marble in places, as soft as a lion cub in others.

She was amazed at how large his arousal was, the sheer magnitude stunning her with its glory. Could they fit together? Could he truly put *that* in *there?* It was so beautiful a thought, the two of them united, that she didn't wish to go beyond it.

Never mind about tomorrow. This was now.

He kissed the corner of her mouth. She repaid him with her tongue, flicking it over his lips. He groaned and whisked it away with his own, exploring the hot cavity of her mouth. He cupped her breasts as they made love with their mouths, and she loved the cool feel of his hands and the sharp burst of heat that seemed to connect her nipples to her thighs.

Drunk with pleasure and desire, she didn't think he could arouse her any more, but he surprised her by tearing away.

"Let me give you a massage."

"But this is—"

"Let me. Please."

With a smile, she complied, lying on her tummy on the towels while he threw another bucket of water on the rocks.

The sound of instant steam roiled through the air. It cradled her in mist, kissed the pockets of her skin that needed moisture, and tripled the sensitivity of her body where he touched her.

He found the mineral oils and kneaded her back. Oh, such wondrous pleasure…superb pulling and tugging at her muscles.

He worked his way from her heels to her toes, pressing each toe and giving it special attention. When he pressed her calves, she thought she'd died and gone to heaven. Then he worked his way up her thighs and she thought surely *then* nothing could feel better, but when his hands reached her buttocks and he massaged the rounded cheeks, she never thought such a feeling of calm and sexual excitement could exist at the same moment.

"You like that?"

He was kneeling above her from the back, and thus she could feel his smooth erection dipping against her thigh.

"Ummm," she answered.

"And this?" He cupped the crease of her bottom and squeezed the muscles.

"Ummm."

"You are so lovely," he whispered in a gravelly voice.

The hands stopped, but her mind was in a faraway place, halfway to the skies and back, trapped in the body of a mortal but feeling as though she could live forever.

Her eyes were closed, for she was surprised by his kiss. He pressed his face to her right breast and kissed the part that was squishing out of the towel at her side. She kept her eyes closed and simply enjoyed the sensation. His mouth on her breast, then on her nipple when she turned slightly to feed it to him.

She was so ready for him, her lifeblood flowing and pumping and heating her.

"Up on your knees…Autumn…."

She wasn't sure what he intended, but she trusted him.

With him still behind her, she rose to her knees and the heels of her hands.

He reached below her and cupped her jiggling breasts. His touch was so sensual, driving her to beg for more, urging him silently to pull and fondle and arouse her nipples till she was so slick and hot she naturally tilted her buttocks toward him.

He rubbed his shaft along her wet folds and she nearly jumped from the pleasure, the excruciating desire to be as one.

She understood. It was a position he was offering, to see how it pleased her.

"Very nice," she murmured in a tease.

Her words seemed to be all the permission he sought. Slowly, he rubbed more and more of himself along her private area, then planted a firm hand on each buttock and guided himself in.

Ohhh…it was wonderful…. He filled her up to the very brim, stretching her around himself, pumping in and out of her in the ancient rhythm of the gods.

There was moaning, and she realized it was coming from her. She was unbridled from restraint, unashamed of her body, proud of her union with Quinn and unbelievably in awe.

He surprised her again. Pulling out, he quickly slid in his fingers, perhaps to save her from pregnancy.

She rode his hand, faster and faster, dearer and dearer till the tidal wave hit. Contractions spent her body, clenching and releasing her bottom, expanding her spirit and engulfing her with a passion so strong for Quinn nothing else mattered.

As the twitching stopped, Quinn slowly released his hold and caressed her hips. He gave her spine a feathery kiss, then turned her over on her back.

"I feel like I can't move." She gave him a tender smile. "You've coaxed me into an utter and complete stupor."

He offered one of those charming grins. "We aim to please."

"We?"

"Us men."

"Now you're taking credit for the entire gender?"

"We each have to do what we can to further the interests of the group."

She giggled into his shoulder. His chest brushed against hers, the steamy heat of his skin dewy with the moisture of the room. They were in a cloud, not just the air, but the feeling between them.

There was something here so vital to her being, her feeling of being wanted and cherished and adored.

Kneeling between her legs, he dipped inside her, filling her from the front as he looked into her eyes.

Could she stay like this, bonded to Quinn, for the rest of her life?

Would he want to?

She certainly saw the joy written on his expression, the way his eyebrows tugged together in deep fascination, the dimple of his cheek, the rooted posture of his lips.

He kissed her deeply, wildly, wantonly, and she wrapped her naked self up against his torso. He slid out then in, filling her again with his rock-hard erection, making her stomach quiver with butterflies that he could want her this much, to do this to her. *With* her.

She loved to watch his face, the concentration, the loss of control…. With a moan, he slid on top of her, his shaft on her belly, until he came there in all his majesty.

A magnificent man sharing one glorious morning, with her.

Chapter Sixteen

Naked, Autumn sat on top of Quinn's buttocks as he lay sprawled on his stomach on the linens. She massaged his shoulders and relished the feel of her feminine parts sliding on his rump.

She hadn't looked at her pocket watch, but it was roughly an hour later, and they were still lounging in the sauna. They'd used the soaps and hair lotions to bathe, the fresh towels to dry, and the water tank that had come to a boil was now spewing steam. Because the back wall was open to the valley and the mountains, the air inside was a graceful blend of pure Alaskan oxygen and thick, sensual steam.

She inhaled deeply and rubbed the moist muscles at the base of his neck.

"Hmm…" he said, adrift in his own thoughts.

From the waist up, he was bronzed from the sun. From the waist down, as white as the towels. She loved the combination, the fact that she was allowed to see him in the most personal way a woman could be with a man.

She leaned over his shoulders to whisper in his ear. Her breasts dangled above him and brushed his skin. The sensation in her nipples rocked through her body straight to her center. She marveled at the magic. "At some point, we're going to have to dress and leave."

Playfully, he tried to scoop her breast with a backhand motion. Missed. "Must you spoil the fun?"

"I work tonight. I need to get back and fix my hair and eat dinner, and see if Victoria—"

"I know," he said gently. "I was teasing. Being selfish. I want you to myself all day."

"Quinn, I dropped into the Imperial before I met you on the docks. They've got my name on the schedule and it's all turned out how the Forrestors said. I truly am rehired."

"I'm happy for you, darlin'."

She smiled at the fortunate turn of events. "Mr. Kennedy is out. The Forrestors are in. I hope they don't turn out to be...rotten."

"So far, so good."

"That's true. They've already proven themselves to be honorable. Very kind of them to take me back."

"You're doing *them* a favor. You're the talented singer. It's *you* pulling in all those customers. All they do is provide the chairs."

Her pleasure deepened at his comments. He was such...a chivalrous knight. Protective and helpful and sticking up for her when no one else was. Was that how husbands reacted?

She cleared her throat, rolled to a sitting position beside him and gave him a tap on the behind, refusing to think—to hope—in that direction. "Well, mister?"

"Yes, miss?"

Their endearments were truly silly, but she enjoyed every single one.

She didn't want this to end.

"Hey," he said, rising up beside her. He cupped her chin. "Hey. Why the fallen face?"

She shrugged her shoulders, not realizing she was that transparent. She motioned to the room. "It's like we've been in our own little fairy-tale world. As soon as we step out the door, the ogre comes to life."

"I'll slay him for you."

Such a sweetheart. She kissed his cheek, and, not daring to think too far into the future, reached for her heap of clothes.

Quinn was troubled and could see Autumn was, too. He stuck his legs into his jeans and pulled them on. He watched as she rolled her cotton stockings to midthigh. Naked except for stockings. Such a sexual vision. Shivering breasts, nipples as hard as gold nuggets, tight stomach and behind.

"If you keep looking at me like that, we're never gonna get out of here," she said.

"If you keep *looking* like that, I don't ever wanna go."

She tilted her head in laughter, and he turned away from the vision and found his shirt. But as soon as she leaned over to get her pantaloons, he snuck another peak.

Her breasts jiggled as she dragged the fabric over her thighs. Still adorable. Still aroused him like hell.

He exhaled in a big groan of frustration.

"I can't tell," she said, sliding into her sleeveless camisole, "whether you're happy or frustrated."

"Both, dammit. I can see why Adam took the apple."

She gasped at the blasphemous words. And then sure to God turned crimson as he watched the flood of color rise, perhaps at how pleased she was that she might tempt him in that manner.

"I think you enjoy that you're so tempting...."

She quickly pulled on her brown silky blouse and tucked it into the skirt she had yanked over her pantaloons.

Goodbye thighs, he mused. "Well, at least now I can think."

He did the buttons on his cuffs as she laughed softly, muttering to herself. "Adam and the apple..."

But there were some things that he needed to say.

She collected the towels off the floor and he reached over to help. "Let me do that." He took one from her hand. "Autumn, last night I got word. The gold shipment should be coming down the mountains in about two weeks."

"You got word? From who?"

"A messenger. At the hotel."

"When I was singing?"

"Yes."

"What does this mean? Will you be leaving town?"

"Not yet. My men are positioning themselves around the pass. Getting ready." Quinn blinked. "Except for Harrison."

"Is he all right?"

"Still fighting that fever. They…they left him behind with the captain."

Her eyes lowered over the hair lotions and bar of soap she was tidying on the counter.

He was trusting her with a lot of information, more than he'd divulged in a long time to anyone. But somehow, it felt right.

"I see." She swung around, pressing her backside into the counter, digging her fingers into the wood as she faced him. "What does this mean, Quinn?"

He stepped closer till he was just a breath away. "What happened between us means a lot. I don't want you to think it had no meaning. Making love to you…was powerful. I feel like I could conquer the world when I'm with you."

She gulped. "And…? There's more coming."

"I want to prove myself to you," he said, hoping she'd understand. "I want to prove I'm worthy."

"You are worthy, Quinn." She cupped his face and he rolled his cheek against her palm, kissing it softly.

He continued. This was no game. This was a matter of life and death. "The next couple of weeks will be difficult. If I don't spend as much time with you as you'd like, understand it's not because I don't want to."

Her face strained.

"It's what I need to do."

They said no more, collected their things and carefully left the cabin. Unfortunately, Quinn was unconvinced that what he'd said to her had eased her worries.

Thor Brander was feeling it again. That weight in his chest, the indigestion in his stomach and the struggle to breathe. Then in a flash, it was gone and he wondered how much of it was in his head. He rolled his shoulder from the ache that no longer was, and tacked up another Wanted poster outside the jailhouse. *Just an exaggeration.*

He'd slept on it the wrong way. Last night, the whore he'd been with had fallen over in a drunken stupor and they'd lain there like two alley cats for about an hour before he woke. He chuckled.

Life was good.

He tapped in the last nail and took a look at his handiwork. The yellow card paper looked brand-spanking-new compared to the other dozen or so posters. This one was a fugitive from Washington. The son of a bitch had shot two government officials before disappearing.

Brander had never seen him in these parts.

He took a hard look at the others and his gaze fell on the shaggy-haired bastard named Quinn Rowlan. His face was a pile of whiskers.

Head of the gang. He'd given Brander more trouble than all the rest of them combined. Who the hell did he think he was? Stirrin' up trouble among his men, laying false claim to the trails and refusing to get out of his district. If Brander ever ran into him, he'd take personal pleasure in slitting his throat. Brander would do it just like his pa had taught him with sheep. Bend over them with a good grip on their wool, hold on to their shoulders and plunge the blade.

Simple.

Lots of blood, though. Too much. He'd have to spare his boots, so maybe he'd get someone else to do it.

A nerve twitched in Brander's neck. A pinch to the left side of his shoulder. He rolled the muscles and stared at the dark eyes on the paper that wouldn't let go.

Rowlan's brother was hurt. How hard could it be for Brander's men to find an injured man? Unless he'd already kicked the bucket and they'd had to bury him.

Brander grinned. Wouldn't that be real nice?

But then that seed of desperation took root in his chest again. The panic, the hatred of *not winning*.

"Wittmann!" He roared into the jailhouse.

The two cells were full. Three men, drifters they'd caught on a shooting spree, looked up from their narrow cots and flinched.

"Wittmann, we've got a hangin' to arrange!"

The other prisoner, the greasy one in the corner they'd hauled in last night, stood up on shaky boots. "Sir, you said I'd get a hearing from the judge first."

"So I did, so I did. We'll wait another few days for him to arrive. If one does. If not, I'll be your judge and jury."

The man turned as white as cream. What did Brander care? He was the law in these parts, and this man had cracked the safe at the jewelry store and just as pretty as he pleased, helped himself to someone else's cash.

Without the decency of asking Brander first. That's the part that made his blood churn. A hanging it would be.

For Autumn, the hours crept by at a turtle's pace. She was determined to abide by Quinn's words that he sought some distance not because he wanted it, but because it was necessary to trap Brander.

Quinn hadn't explained it outright, but she was an intelligent woman and understood. If he was being followed by Brander's men, then any time she and Quinn spent together privately would have to involve an energy expenditure in dodging the spies. They'd be taking chances with stolen moments, and all that energy would have to come from somewhere. Quinn would have to take his eyes off his game, to put the well-being of innocents behind his own selfish interests of his love life.

Something he wasn't prepared to do, thought Autumn, torn between admiration for Quinn and her own selfish desires.

She couldn't fault him for putting his brother's and

the town's interests above his own. She repeated it in her mind as she entered the stage for her first evening under the new hotel management. She couldn't fault him. Yet, it hurt.

Thunderous applause went out to her beneath a packed house, with the two Forrestor men clapping loudest at the back. Quinn watched from the bar, silently lifting his shot glass in salute when the night was over and the money counted for her cut of the beverages. An entire twenty-two dollars and thirty cents. Money she couldn't believe was hers. Back home, a good day's wage for a healthy man was a dollar a day.

The following days were spent in much the same manner. Up early for breakfast, a nice chat with Victoria, shopping at the market for the latest tins of fresh fruit, then more singing.

But not more of Quinn.

Autumn tried not to be too disappointed, and allowed him the space to make his plans. She watched as he maneuvered himself around Brander, who came in most nights to listen to her entertainment. She wondered what was being said on Saturday then Monday night again when Quinn spoke with the Russian sea captain in hushed tones, and later on Wednesday evening to a man he introduced her to as the banker. The crooked banker.

"Evening, Mr. Shackleford," she told him after a particularly strong rendition of "Oh My Darling, Clementine."

"Miss MacNeil. Congratulations on your success."

"Thank you."

"Have a seat." Quinn pulled out a stool beside him at the bar. Appreciative, she brushed his shoulder with her hand as she slid onto it. Honest to God, it was the first time she'd touched him in a week. Their eyes met. He quickly averted his.

There was no time like the present, she thought, eyeing Shackleford, a thin buzzard of a man who was pecking at his battered whitefish. Complimentary food. Land's sake, why did the people who could most afford things always get them free?

She gave the banker a gracious smile. "You're new to Skagway, Mr. Shackleford. I imagine you do a great deal of business here."

"A lot of folks are here to fulfill a dream."

"Have you noticed all the women who are doing well?"

He shrugged. "Haven't really set my mind to it."

"There's a dear friend of mine who started a sandwich shop last year. She's earned over ten thousand dollars."

That spun the man's head.

"And that journalist from Boston who's taking photographs and shipping everything to her publisher, compiling notes for the state colleges."

"She must be broke," said Shackleford with a despicable grunt of a laugh.

Autumn took a deep breath and pushed the insult aside. She'd heard them so often, she'd learned it was no use arguing with a pig.

She continued undaunted, proud of her fellow sisters. "One of the jewelers in town died six months ago and left his shop to his daughter. She tripled the business when she decided to craft jewelry directly from gold nuggets. She has that way with her hands. Then there's Bessy-Sue, who opened the laundry on the first corner past Main. She brought soap from her hometown of New Orleans that makes her laundry smell extra-sweet. And of course, you know Miss Flora with her saunas."

Autumn had lost the banker's attention. She could see it in the way his eyes faded and he looked past her shoulder to the stage, where Cornelius was about to sing some of his famous opera tunes.

"And so I wondered if you'd be interested in loaning me some money," she whispered, knowing he was no longer listening. "You see, I have this dream...."

The man yawned in the direction of the stage. He wasn't even looking at her anymore.

She blinked away the sting of humiliation.

The banker may have turned away, but Quinn was still riveted on her face.

The kindness she saw etched in the furrows around his mouth made her stomach clench. He knew what this meant to her. He felt the expectation, the hope.

Quinn didn't wallow for long in the moment. He turned to the banker.

"Have another drink," Quinn said to the man, ordering a round of Scotch while winking at Autumn.

If she couldn't get the man to bankroll her hotel, she'd at least get a portion of his liquor sales tonight.

Autumn smiled at the absurdity. The pent-up frustration she felt released at witnessing Quinn's schoolboy tactics of getting even.

Quinn walked her home but was careful to keep his distance, and the topic of conversation to a nonpersonal nature.

For Autumn, the second week was even harder than the first. The time was drawing nearer for the gold shipment to be coming around the cliffs, but no one was letting her in on any of the details. Quinn still walked her home occasionally, but he always signaled that someone was behind them, watching every move. He didn't dare lean in for a kiss, let alone scoop her into his arms and carry her into any sauna, or make love to her as though it was his last breath on earth.

The loneliness reminded her how she'd felt when the doctor had come out of her grandpa's bedroom and she could see in that instant, by the sorrowful expression, that her grandpa had just passed away.

And then just a short while later, it seemed, her grandma had died of heart failure. A broken heart, that same doctor had declared, from being separated from the man she'd shared fifty-three years with.

Autumn trudged along the boardwalk on the following Tuesday, protecting herself from the hot sun with her straw hat and wondered.

Would anyone ever share fifty-three years with her?

A commotion kicked up at the end of the street,

close to the harbor. She moved to the railing and strained to see above the turning bonnets and Stetsons.

Her stomach shook. Her nerves flew. Something about the gold shipment? Dear Lord, was someone hurt?

Then just as bold as you please, six riders on weathered horses reared up beside the Imperial Hotel. Straight across from where she was standing. Trouble at the hotel?

Folks began to hoot and holler in *her* direction. Why?

She struggled to disappear into the crowd when she spotted the broad cowboy hat, then familiar face, of Gilbert Oakley.

After two weeks of a fruitless search to God knew where, they were back. The posse—her posse—was back in town.

If pressed, she'd have to lie to these kind gentlemen about what truly happened on the eve of her disappearance. Her hips ground into the doorway of the mercantile as she stepped backward, trying to fade into oblivion. But the crowd parted around her, giving an opportunity for the men of the posse to step forward and confront her. How utterly embarrassing.

Chapter Seventeen

Quinn was on his way to the Imperial Hotel when he noticed the ruckus and the returning posse. He pushed through the hot bodies on the boardwalk, then saw Autumn retreating across the street. Was she good at fibbing? Could she look boldly at her own posse, likely men who admired and respected her, and lie straight into their eyes?

No time to figure it out. Quinn rushed across the street and joined her side.

"Miss MacNeil," he said, tilting his Stetson in a howdy gesture.

He was dressing like a businessman these days—black denims, spiffed up with a white business shirt and his fringed suede jacket.

Creases around her eyes relaxed at seeing him. She pushed back her shoulders and stepped forward to greet her would-be liberators.

"Gilbert Oakley," she said to a strapping, dark-haired man who was looking at her dumbfounded. "Nice to see you."

Quinn had heard the name. The man was one of the town's best locksmiths.

Gilbert took off his cowboy hat and slapped his thigh with it. His holsters, heavy with gun weight, shifted. "I couldn't believe when I heard. You're safe."

"Yes…yes, thank you."

"What's going on?" Quinn would play the role of her innocent business partner. "Who are these men?"

Autumn toyed with her lips. "The posse."

"Well," said Quinn, trying to inject humor. "Nice to see you boys are back."

Gilbert frowned, maybe a bit disgruntled that he'd come this far for nothing. "I thought…I thought they took you."

"Hmm?" She raised her slender eyebrows in total innocence. "No, no, I'm here."

"Where were you?"

She rolled her tongue beneath her bottom lip. "With him." She nodded at Quinn. It wasn't a lie. She had been with him.

Gilbert turned his focus on Quinn. "And you are?"

"Her business advisor. An investor."

Another of the six men stepped forward and stared at Autumn. "But we thought you were kidnapped!"

Then another added, "Snatched at midnight, by God knows who!"

Autumn colored fiercely. "It may have looked like

that…and I'm terribly sorry to have burdened you all. I truly appreciate that you went out to find me."

She gave Gilbert a most pleasing smile, which Quinn didn't find so pleasing.

There was something more private going on between the two that rankled Quinn. He had no business claiming her, though. How could he claim a woman he couldn't give his name to?

"Thank you, Gilbert." Quinn peered down at him.

Gilbert shuffled uneasily with the words. Maybe it was the cool tone of Quinn's voice that chafed the man. Hell, Quinn hadn't meant to give anything away in regard to his own private feelings for Autumn.

She shot Quinn a disapproving look.

What the hell was Quinn supposed to do? Shake the hand of every man who wanted this woman in bed? That'd be the whole blasted town! Even Brander was making his moves—she might not have noticed, but Quinn was aware every time the slimy reptile flicked his tongue in her direction.

Trying to come to grips with his jealousy, Quinn addressed the other men. "You've done a fine job, gentlemen. I'd have to take the blame for her disappearance, so to speak."

Autumn threw another heated look in his direction.

Quinn's mouth tugged upward. It was sort of humorous, him explaining. The posse was staring at the very man they'd been looking for, for two weeks.

"Tell you what. After you check in with the deputy

marshal, if you head on over to the Skagway Arms, lunch and drinks are on me. Jim Windsor."

The men seemed a bit conflicted. They'd lost two weeks of their time for nothing, it seemed, and the damsel in distress hadn't been in distress at all. But in all seriousness, Quinn was beholden to each one of them. Men like these made the frontier safer.

Autumn stepped off the platform to thank each one of them individually. She gave the man Gilbert a kiss on the cheek. Quinn ground his jaw and turned away.

"Rode to Dyea," said Gilbert.

"Then over to the White Pass trail," explained another.

"Back down to the other side. To the inlet where the ocean begins."

"No sign of you at all, Miss MacNeil."

She whispered back soothing words, and promises that she'd never forget them for their bravery.

And then as they turned away to head to the jailhouse, another commotion kicked up. Two of Brander's deputies came riding in on horseback, galloping in a cloud of dust, one of them hauling a man slumped over the back of his horse.

Even at the distance of a block away, Quinn could see the prisoner's hands were tied together.

A familiar tan vest. Head of loose brown hair.

Quinn's gut jerked. Lord, no...

He started breathing hard. His instinct kicked in

and he jumped off the boardwalk, striding at full pace toward the man.

The closer he got, the faster his heart pounded.

No, please… But hanging limply on the back of the horse, almost unconscious, was his brother.

Brander heard the shouting and the thunder of hooves from inside the jailhouse.

"What the hell?" He jumped up to the door, taking his rifle with him.

The men in the cells stood up from their cots. Even they could sense trouble in the air.

As Brander stepped through the door, he moved to the boardwalk in front of his Wanted posters. A crowd was accumulating around him. Everyone was interested in fresh meat. They always were, whether it was a hanging or a shooting. Or this. A good-for-nothin' son of a bitch tied to the back of a mare.

Kendrick and Wittmann came to a halt at the hitching post and sprang down.

"Who you got?" With his blood pulsing with excitement, Brander slowly stepped off the boardwalk. His boots and spurs jangled in the dirt.

Kendrick smiled as though he'd won a jackpot. "Harrison Rowlan."

Brander's spit crackled, his eyes sharpened like an eagle's. "That so?"

Cocking his rifle, he eased in closer to the weakened son of a bitch. The man, eyes closed, dangled like a rag doll three feet off the ground.

A wonder of epic proportion engulfed Brander. A grin stretched his lips so tight all he could do was nod. And examine the specimen.

He looked past the scruffy black beard and the greasy forehead. Perspiration was pouring from the man's temples, drizzling down the bridge of his brows to the ground.

"Where was he hidin'?"

"The fishing village. One of our guys got a message last night."

The crowd was silent, but the shift of boots was loud. One set in particular, boots thudding in a running rhythm on the boardwalk, suddenly stopped just above him. Brander looked up to see Jim Windsor, a mass of muscle and sinew, standing shoulders spread beside the Wanted posters.

"Who is it?" Jim seemed mighty tense. His eyes were flashing and he was standing there twitching, as if ready for a fight.

"Fella we been after for a while." Brander nodded to the drawing behind the investor. "That's his picture there."

Windsor didn't turn around, though. Other folks did, but not him.

"Wanted for robbing a shipping line," Brander explained. "Killed two women on their way down to the river two months ago. They might have been prostitutes, but they had rights, too."

"Witnesses?"

"Got plenty of those."

"Who?"

Why was the man so interested? A fly buzzed around the investor's shoulder and landed on a poster behind his back. Brander's eyes flicked over the sketch of Quinn Rowlan. Then back to Windsor.

Something wasn't right. Brander sensed it in his gut. Slowly, he anchored his finger on the trigger of his rifle.

"Get the prisoner down," Brander shouted to Kendrick and Wittmann. "Haul him to a cell."

When Brander looked up again, the MacNeil woman was inching toward Windsor on the boardwalk, eyes riveted on the prisoner. Her face was pale, lips trembling. A woman of this sensitivity didn't often see the darker side of the world. The crime and ignorance.

Brander wanted to shield her from it. "Best step away," he said, then turned to everyone else. "Give us some space to pass through."

But Windsor wouldn't step back. The others did—in fact the MacNeil woman tried to tug him at the elbow—but he looked like he wanted to take a gander at the criminal.

Kendrick kicked the unconscious man off the horse. He fell to the ground with a thud, hands still bound, feet in chains, and groaned.

Windsor cursed and leaped forward.

Brander stopped him with the length of his rifle. "No need to help."

Kendrick took the arms and Wittmann took his

legs, and they dragged that vermin along the dirt, just barely lifting his body off the stones. His eyes opened and closed with his moans. His torso was wrapped in bloody strips of linen.

As he passed Windsor, the prisoner's eyes opened. Windsor looked down, his jaw tense, his nostrils flared. Seemed to Brander the man was a sissy. How could he be so moved at the sight of a criminal in shackles?

"Quinn," the prisoner croaked, barely audible, but Brander heard it loud and clear and it was like a knife scraping down his spine. "Quinn."

Suddenly, for Brander, it all kicked into place.

Windsor went for his guns, hit Kendrick in the mouth with a backhand and smashed Wittmann in the gut. But Brander's finger was already on his rifle. Didn't take much to lift and aim.

"Well, now," Brander said calmly, among the crowd's screaming. He looked back and forth from the Wanted poster to the man panting before him. Same dark eyes, mole above his left eyebrow, turn of his nose and chin. "We got two for one."

With fingers trembling into her skirts, never having been this close to a gun aimed at someone she cared about, Autumn stepped up beside Quinn. She confronted Brander. "I demand you treat this man with—"

Brander gave her a cold, hard look and she clamped her mouth shut. He was liable to shoot them all. Yet…had he pieced together that she was in cahoots with Quinn? As far as Brander knew, she thought Quinn truly *was* Jim Windsor.

"Lock him up!" Brander ordered Kendrick, and it caused her throat to quiver. Her limbs froze. She had to *do* something—anything—but her boots wouldn't move.

The crowd broke into a frenzy.

"It's the outlaw!"

"Shoot him now!"

"And his dirty brother!"

Quinn gave her a pleading look, his dark eyes racked with fury at Brander, but sympathy and concern for her. Everything about his stance begged her to back off, from the step he took away from her, to the way his chin dipped downward, to the reclining pose of his hands.

Stay put. Let them take me and save yourself.

Maybe knowing he had other townsfolk as witnesses, Kendrick held his rage in check, but approached Quinn with all the pent-up venom of having just been punched in the face. He thrust his revolver into Quinn's back, growled and shoved him toward the jailhouse.

Quinn, stoic and determined to retain his dignity, lifted his unconscious brother off the ground and carried him, hands and feet shackled, toward the door as though Quinn were lifting a wounded animal.

Autumn's heart shattered at the sight.

This man had sacrificed more than any other to do what he felt was right for mere *strangers,* and he'd been repaid with disgust and dishonor.

How could she help him?

Brander was close enough that she could lift one of the rocks off the street and smash the side of his face. Or she might dive for his gun and blast a hole through that shriveled heart.

Yet still her legs felt like anchors. She realized the ideas flying out of her head were temporary solutions to a problem that would land them all in jail.

She needed to find a better solution, one that could help them permanently.

Her mind grew dizzy, her mouth dry as a board. Weakness set in when what she prayed for was strength.

The cold hand of time seemed to stand still as the deputy marshal and his two assailants strode into the jailhouse, following Quinn. Roman gladiators hungry for a kill. Quinn disappeared, the door banged closed and Autumn flinched as though her face had just been smacked.

Autumn's waiting didn't get any easier. She rushed to find Victoria, but she was out on a medical call. Hours later, they finally met up in the parlor of their home.

"I'm so sorry," Victoria whispered as she removed her shawl. "You care about Quinn a great deal."

The truth of that statement left Autumn empty of words. But she wasn't able to confess just how deep her feelings went, or how intimate the two of them had been. "Quinn's men need to be told."

"But you don't know where they are."

"Someone out there must realize Harrison is missing."

"That's right," said Victoria, her voice softening. "They'll band together and free Quinn *and* Harrison."

But the soothing remarks sat awkward between them. They were limp hopes, when both women knew time was not on their side. Autumn forced herself to think clearly, and for that, she had to face some awful facts.

"Deputy Marshal is already planning one hanging."

"Gracious," said Victoria. "Who?"

"The man who robbed the jewelry store."

"They don't hang folks for stealing."

"Maybe not most lawmen." Autumn paced the floor, around the sofa to the windowpane and view of the mountains. "But I heard he found some evidence the thief brutally stabbed some folks on the trail. Now he's up on murder charges."

"Did he do it?"

"Quinn seems to think it's two gold miners Brander himself is responsible for."

Victoria planted both hands at the back of her neck and walked the floor.

Finally, Victoria stated what they were both thinking but neither found easy to say. "You're worried they'll hang Quinn."

"As sure as I'm standing here, I know they'll try." Autumn swallowed back the terror in her throat.

There was a desperation in her belly that seemed bottomless. Quinn was facing death, his brother was hurting something bad, no one in town believed the truth, Brander was getting away with murder and she...she had no way to lift herself out of this hole and simply be with the man she adored.

Chapter Eighteen

Quinn found it difficult to sit by Harrison's cot and do nothing. He'd lost weight in the two weeks since Quinn had last seen him. Pale, his cheek bones protruding from the weight loss, Harrison snored loudly. Quinn nudged him gently on the shoulder.

"Harrison, can you hear me?"

He mumbled in his sleep. "Yeah…good seein'…" He trailed off, but Quinn was grateful that it was sleep and not a coma.

Another man looked on, weary and listless himself, clutching at the bars, watching Quinn's every move.

"What're you in for?" Quinn asked him.

The man shook his head. "Not what he says I did."

Quinn rose, seething once again at Brander, who was hiding somewhere in the other room. Two other men looked on from the far cell, squinting through half-closed eyes, one on each cot. They were greasy, unshaven and smelled like sour whiskey. Drunks.

"I'm Quinn Rowlan," he said to his cell mate.

"Mutt Stanley."

"Know anything about medicine?"

"No, sir. I'm a… I was a… I wasn't much of anything, to tell ya the truth."

Quinn stepped past him and hollered into the pit of the jail, toward the front room where he knew the lizard was hiding.

"My brother needs a nurse!"

A jangle of spurs hit the floor. Quinn couldn't see anything, then a big black boot appeared in the doorway, along with the rest of him. Brander.

"Reckon I'd like one of those pretty gals myself."

Quinn wanted to beat the living tar out of him, but hours had passed in the cell, the dinner hour had come and gone without a morsel for any of them, and he was trapped.

He swallowed past his pride. "You're a man of the law. A decent, civil man. I need someone who knows something about medicine."

"Well, two of the nurses are still outta town, and I reckon Miss MacNeil is so disgusted with you right now, her friend Miss Windhaven doesn't want anything to do with you. Matter of fact, I was just about to go pay my regards to the miss." Brander squinted at him. "How'd you like a surgeon, though? I heard one just arrived on a ship."

Quinn faltered. "Surgeon would do fine."

Brander roared with glee. "Goddamn surgeon. Right." His words were filled with sarcasm.

Liar.

"I'd like to speak to a lawyer."

Brander drew closer. "Would you now?"

"I know there's a law office two blocks over."

"They left yesterday for the Klondike. Seems even the lawyers are clawing their way to gold."

Quinn didn't believe it. He'd seen the men through the window just yesterday morning, working on papers.

"When's the judge coming?"

Brander scoffed and laughed some more, heading back to the front room from where he'd come. Leaving Quinn with a deep black hole in the pit of his stomach.

No gun to defend himself. No knife. No food.

Hell. He turned around and paced back to the middle of his cell. The other men were watching from the corners of their eyes. Quinn sank into the cot beside his brother's feet.

A banging from outside the cell hammered into his mind, along with thoughts of escape. He didn't have to look to see what the carpenters were working on.

Two more nooses to add to the one they were already planning. He looked over at his brother and nearly wept.

There had to be an opportunity. Some small detail Quinn was overlooking. Some law he could toss in Brander's face, someone in town who'd listen to their story and sympathize. He took mental note of every item in the cell, grappling with how he might use it as a tool. Two wooden cots—for three men—put together with nails, two straw mattresses, two blankets and one piss pot. And a plank floor built right over the dirt.

He thought of Autumn and knew she was likely doing all she could, but how much would that amount to? Better off if she never came back to him. Never set foot in the jailhouse, pretended like she never knew him. He couldn't stomach the thought of…any hair on her head coming to harm.

The rest of his men, Jackson and Ben and Trevor and Vic, were so dependable, Quinn knew they were just where they were supposed to be. Miles away in the mountains, waiting to protect the gold miners if they were ambushed. Except…who had been looking after Harrison? What had happened to that man? Had Brander's deputy shot him on the spot?

Which one of Quinn's men might be dead?

An hour later, Quinn tried to rouse his brother. Mercifully, the jailers had brought a jug of fresh water, but still no food.

The nailing and sawing outside hadn't let up. Quinn stood up, about to holler, when the sound of petticoats rustling and whispered female voices made him reel toward the office.

After a moment, the women walked in. Victoria and Autumn.

As shocked as Quinn was to see them, he stood up and kept his mouth shut.

Brander escorted them in, or more like followed

them as though trying to stop them. Victoria looked straight at Quinn, lashes fluttering with nerves. Autumn kept her gaze to the floor. Both ladies were dressed in fine clean blouses and skirts. Pretty hats adorned their hair.

Between them, Victoria carried a medicine bag and Quinn inhaled in a huge whoop of joy.

"Now I urge you," Victoria said to the deputy marshal, "to let me in there."

Brander tugged her back by the arm. "Not so fast."

For a moment, Autumn flinched. Then her lips tightened into a line and Quinn could almost see the steam rising from her collar.

Quinn stepped up to the cell wall. "The penal code says prisoners are allowed medical services, should the need arise."

"Shut up," growled Brander.

"Furthermore, three meals a day."

"Shut *up*," Brander barked. "Who the hell do you think you are? This is *my* jailhouse. *My* town. *My* rules. Got that?"

Autumn softened her stance toward Brander. "*I* told her she shouldn't come. I told her she was making a big mistake."

Quinn tilted his head, trying to fathom what was going on. Autumn had yet to look at him, so he couldn't decide. She was putting on an act, wasn't she?

Victoria yanked her arm free of Brander, but she stepped back. "I'll do as you ask, Deputy Marshal. I was thinking, however, that you might like to have this man stand up and *walk* to the gallows. How would it look if you hanged a sick man?"

Quinn gulped hard. Where was this leading? He tingled with expectation, the desire for Brander to take out his goddamn keys and unlock the cell.

Brander weighed the decision. "Kendrick!"

Kendrick darted out from the office.

"Take out your gun and swing it this way," said Brander. "Aim it for the big one, here, right between his eyes as I unlock the cell. If he so much as breathes the wrong way, shoot him."

Quinn stood as still as a watchful hawk. He stepped back from the door so as not to startle anyone, and sat, fuming, on the other cot beside Stanley.

The one and only thing he wanted to come of this right now was that Harrison got help.

Victoria walked inside, skirts swirling as she kneeled beside Harrison and unbuttoned what was left of his dirty shirt. Working quickly, she unbuckled her medical bag, removed a stethoscope, some gauze padding and an antiseptic.

Listening to his heart with her instruments, Victoria concentrated on her task. Finally. Finally Harrison was getting the help he needed, but was it too late?

Quinn vowed not to think like that. He watched Victoria unwind the crusty old bandages, watched Harrison wince as she soaked the wound with her tonics, watched her take a blade and scrape something out of the wound as Harrison shuddered in agony.

Autumn turned away then, too, but refused to look at Quinn.

He played along. Or, if it wasn't an act, he silently agreed he'd caused her a heap of misery.

The jail block grew hot from the bodies waiting and watching. Beads of sweat rolled down Quinn's temples, but he didn't dare move his hand to wipe them for fear of being shot.

When it was all done, maybe thirty minutes in total, when Harrison's torso was bound in clean gauze and was beginning to simmer from the morphine tablet she'd given him, the ladies turned to leave. Autumn still refused to look.

Victoria handed Quinn a small bottle of liquid. "Give him a mouthful every six hours. It'll help with the fever and the pain."

Quinn studied her kind expression and held out his hand, unsure if she'd take it. With a slight hesitation, she did.

"I'm mighty obliged. Thank you, Miss Windhaven."

She nodded goodbye and turned to follow Autumn out of the cell.

"Wait," Quinn said to Autumn, talking through the bars.

Kendrick cocked his trigger and the loud click rattled through the air and down Quinn's spine.

"Easy," said Brander. "Don't you try nothin'."

Autumn finally lifted her eyes to his. They were steeled against him, hard and aloof.

"A doomed man's last wish?" he said to her.

"What's that?"

"I'd like to be buried properly. Will you see to it?"

Her eyes glistened with moisture. Her throat moved up and down. She was masking a great *deal* of emotion, he just wished he knew what it was.

"All right," she said calmly.

"Means I need to be sized up for a proper casket."

Brander squawked some sort of laugh, and Kendrick motioned for her to leave the cell.

She moved aside and the cell door slammed with the loud clatter of heavy iron.

With a heavy thud in his chest, Quinn watched her leave.

Autumn struggled to contain all the feelings she was suppressing as she and Victoria left the jailhouse and headed down the boardwalk.

"Slow down a bit. You're walking too fast," Victoria said, indicating they didn't want to attract attention.

Autumn slowed her steps. Her boots pounded crisply on the wooden planks. They nodded to passing folks. It was agony before they turned the corner and she was able to express what she felt. Seeing Quinn all caged up like that had made her nauseated. Had stoked the anger she felt toward Brander and his cowardly men. She felt a determination to rip those bars apart herself if she had to.

"I know what he was telling me," Autumn said to her friend. "I know what he was telling me!" Optimism raced through her.

"Shh," said Victoria, stepping around the corner building as two men exited the café.

It was well after the dinner hour, but because the summer sun was limitless in the sky, some shops remained open twenty-four hours. If one had enough gold dust, he or she could shop forever.

Autumn reminded herself there could be enemies in their midst—men who answered to Brander. She took a look behind her. All clear. Ahead…no one. "We're not going home."

"Where to, then?"

"Gilbert's."

"Why? Is that what Quinn was telling you?"

"Not exactly. That part I thought of on my own."

"Explain."

"Quinn was telling me the casket would be his opportunity. That's all. An opportunity for him to try something."

"But what?"

"I'm not sure exactly what he has in mind. But *I* can think of one thing."

"What?"

"Follow me." Making sure they weren't being followed, Autumn darted into the alleyway, past another, dipped past the mercantile with its closed door, through the stalls of the livery stables and out, finally, to see the one person she hoped would accept her apology and give her what she needed. She stepped up silently to the back door, and as she knocked on the heavy slab, she prayed he was home.

* * *

The medication was working. Quinn watched the steady rhythm of Harrison's breathing and for the first time in a long while, he found comfort. His brother was finally, truly, on the mend. If he could just get strong enough to stand on his feet, he and Quinn could get out of this. Together.

It was very early morning, hours since he'd last seen Autumn's face. The other men in the hold were sound asleep—Harrison, Stanley and the two others snoring three yards over. Quinn walked to the cold bars and listened for signs of life. The lonely sound of animals drifted in from the window. Frogs and crickets and night owls. The call of a moose. Then the tinny sound of piano music and banjos drifted over from the line of saloons along the shoreline.

Would he ever drink in a saloon again?

He stepped to the end of Harrison's cot, found a spot around his brother's feet, leaned back against the bars and nodded off thinking of Autumn. The feel of her lips. The soft turn of her mouth, the proud twist of her shoulders when Kennedy had fired her, the melodic sound of her soft voice as she sang of home and country.

It must've been a couple of hours later when he awoke to the sound of keys jangling and boots coming his way. He started, his neck pinched from sitting up against the bars.

Brander hollered, "Someone here to meet you!"

A stranger walked beside him, a man with thin dark hair and reluctant walk, more of a shuffle, as though apologetic.

What was Brander so pleased about?

Quinn's gut tightened. Couldn't be good.

"Get up," Brander snarled as he came to their cell. "You need to be measured."

The casket maker. Quinn's heart pounded. He nudged his brother. Groggy though he was, Harrison opened his eyes fully and blinked. There was recognition in his dark eyes.

Thank the Lord, Harrison was back. Quinn helped him rise. As pleased as Quinn was about Harrison's apparent recuperation, Quinn had to give him some bad news.

"What is it?" asked Harrison. His hair was mussed up at the side of his head, and he badly needed a shave. He could also use a bath. Harrison took in his position in the jail cell, and whether he remembered the circumstances of his being here or not, he remained quiet, taking direction from Quinn.

"Need to be measured for a casket."

"What the hell…"

Mutt Stanley jolted awake, shot up like a bolt of lightning and screamed.

The sound pierced the quiet. The other two prisoners rolled over in their cots. Quinn surmised they were awake, but had decided to lie low for their own safety.

"Calm down," Quinn told Stanley. "Calm down."

"You calm down! I ain't doin' this!"

The casket maker spoke softly. "You don't need to, mister. I can guess your size."

This upset Stanley even more.

It wasn't so much fear that clawed at Quinn's throat, but rage at what Brander was doing in this fine country.

"It'll take me a couple of days to get the pine boxes cut."

"Hurry," said Brander. "We'll be needin' 'em sooner than later."

Stanley screamed again.

Quinn looked down at the small packet of tools the casket maker had set down on the cot. Pencil, measuring tape, a small stack of rosary beads. Quinn's brow broke out into a sweat. Nothing else? Nothing? He examined the man's body. Belt buckle. No guns, obviously. Nothing in his shirt pocket.

Hadn't Autumn got the message? Hadn't she understood? Or was she just unable to do anything with it?

When the measuring was completed, with Brander and Kendrick still leaning against the wall, Quinn spotted it.

He tried real hard not to smile. She had come through.

"These are yours," said the casket maker, lifting out three rungs of rosary beads. "Courtesy of the nurse and her friend. If you want 'em." He looked to Brander for permission. The deputy marshal scowled but didn't object.

Quinn accepted his and so did Harrison, but Stanley, still on the bed, kicked the floor with his boots. "I don't want one!"

Quinn wasn't paying much attention to Stanley, for his eyes were riveted on the toolbox. There in the bottom of the crate, slipped into the top between the planks, was what looked to be a key. Key to a jail cell? It was elongated and shiny, as if newly cut, and Quinn would bet his heart that she'd gone to Gilbert Oakley to have one cut special.

How was he supposed to reach it, though? He'd be shot by Kendrick, who was still holding a gun on them. The burning need to escape gripped Quinn and crackled through the air.

"Get that bastard outta here!" Stanley shouted at the casket maker.

"Shut up!" Kendrick came at him with a gun, Brander came up real close to the bars in a menacing stance, and that's when Stanley made his unexpected move.

He dove for the urinal, lifted the sloshing pot and flung it at Brander. It hit the iron bars with a huge clang and Brander got covered in piss.

Brander squealed like it was acid. "Goddamn!"

With everyone in an uproar, Quinn slid his hand into the casket maker's toolbox and yanked out the key. Harrison stood up slowly from the cot, ashen.

Quinn looked up in time to see Brander raise his gun and blast Stanley in the gut. His buckled body slammed against the bars, bleeding.

Quinn lunged out of the cell at Brander. Harrison dove over the casket maker and tackled Kendrick.

Guns flew to the ground.

"Here, mister, here!" shouted the prisoners in the other cell. "Kick a gun over here!"

The casket maker scurried around the fighting men and disappeared. Quinn pounded Brander's jaw, but Brander got him back and slugged him hard in the gut. Quinn crashed against the wall, then lunged again, driving his fist into Brander's stomach. Brander doubled over, huffing for breath.

"The gun!" the prisoners called. "Kick it!"

No time for that. Quinn had the better of Brander, but he heard Harrison moan. Quinn looked over and Kendrick was pummeling his brother's face.

Quinn jumped over to help, kicking Kendrick hard in the back of the leg.

Brander, close to the door, made a run for it, leaving Quinn with the decision of helping his brother or chasing the son of a bitch down the street.

Without hesitation, Quinn knocked Kendrick in the jaw. He heard a loud crack, and Kendrick fell to the ground.

Harrison, his bandages soaked with fresh blood, needed help to get to his feet.

"You all right?" Quinn hollered. "You all right?"

"Yeah." They both looked to the empty doorway, then heard the sound of a horse galloping away.

Quinn flung the key from his pocket to the men

in the other jail cell. "Help Stanley," he said. "Get him to the nurse. He's still breathing."

The men leaped to do as they were asked.

It wasn't quite how Quinn had planned it. If Stanley had only been a bit more patient, Quinn could've gotten them all out unharmed. Autumn's gift of a key would've done it.

Quinn kicked Kendrick over with one big boot, took his handcuffs and shackled his wrists. "Take this deputy here," he added to the prisoners who were racing to unlock their cells, "and jail him. Tell the lawyers down the street what you've done. Tell them Brander's the outlaw, not me."

Quinn turned to his younger brother. "Come on. We've got something to finish."

Chapter Nineteen

Quinn dug his boots into the side of his horse and rode as fast as a brushfire catching to dry wood. The warm Alaskan wind ruffled his hair, the sun beat down on his Stetson and the muscles of his mare clenched and released beneath his thighs. Last week at the livery stables, he'd rented the horse, and the spare Harrison was riding, and had them on hand in case the need should arise.

Harrison was barely keeping up beside Quinn, but had insisted Quinn ride full out, across the Lynn Canal, past the town of Dyea, up the mountain toward the Chilkoot Trail. Harrison had explained as best he could that Jackson had been shot in the leg and left behind by the two men on Brander's dirty payroll.

This left Trevor in charge, with Ben and Vic behind. Not many men to ward off the ones Brander had surely hired for his last big haul through the mountains.

"You sure Brander came this way?" Harrison

shouted close to noon, after they'd stopped to chew down some jerky they'd bought across from the livery.

"If he already had enough gold to make him happy, he would've left town by now. Means he intends this to be his last heist. He can't go back to the jailhouse. But he's got that Russian Captain at his disposal to set sail for home, whenever he snaps his fingers."

"You sure figured out a lot on your own."

"Wasn't by myself."

"Who with?"

"Autumn MacNeil."

Harrison said nothing, but cocked his head in that brotherly way Quinn remembered from their youth, the one that meant "whatever you say, but I find that hard to believe."

Harrison downed some of the liquid the nurse had given him, and swigged a mouthful of water from his canteen. "You smell awful."

Quinn had bought the clean white shirt off the stable hand's back, but his pants were still stained from fighting with Brander, who'd been soaked in urine.

"Not as bad as you."

Harrison frowned, looked up from his canteen and the two brothers shared a grin. Old times.

"It's good to have you back." Quinn jumped onto his saddle.

"Good to breathe again." Harrison hopped onto his mare, protecting his injured side.

They rode hard. Passed a few empty-handed miners

along the way. Two hours up the cliffs, and down a hidden trail beyond the main one, before they caught sight of what they were looking for. A battalion of men, it seemed, coming in through a narrow pass in the gully below, hauling chest after chest of heavy material.

"Gold," whispered Harrison, thunderstruck.

"We're not the only ones who see them." Quinn looked around from his perch, but saw no one hidden in the trees. Brander and his hired guns had to be somewhere. And where were Quinn's men?

"Now what?" asked Harrison.

Quinn leaned forward on his saddle horn. "We wait and follow."

Brander tried not to think of this morning in the jailhouse as he choked back on his canteen. Water dribbled down his chin. His chest felt like it was on fire, that was how deep the rage bore down on him. To hell with Rowlan. And his goddamn sickly brother. Brander hoped both of them would rot with the devil.

He'd outwitted them all. His chest swelled with glory at the magnificent sight below, in the gully. Ten gold miners on mules, horseback or on foot were hauling such heavy trunks they likely only covered two or three miles a day. Four other men rode on horseback, likely hired guards.

Every last man who'd ever crossed Brander would soon hear the tale of the smartest man in Alaska.

Flanked by eight of the best shooters in Skagway, Brander gave his signal to slow down and wait for his order to charge. Back up, he motioned to them. He wanted to head back down the trail and wait till they got into more of a clearing. There'd be a lot of gunfire and he didn't want anyone slipping away with any gold. His men did as he asked, moving down five hundred yards. Across the gully, on the other edge of the cliff, Brander caught a glimmer of something white. A shirt? He peered closer.

Nothing.

The waiting was killing him. On his orders, Yuri and his six crewmates had already set sail for the southern coast, to dock beyond the village of Kirkland. Now, here, Brander had the wagons ready, along with the extra horses.

He eyed the woods. Nothing coming yet. It was too soon. He took another swig of water, imagining what Deborah might say when he appeared at her door, a brand-new millionaire.

"Oh, how dashing you look, Thor." She'd smile and invite him in for ice—

A gunshot snapped him out of it. Brander reeled to the woods. "Not yet! Not yet!"

But it was too late. Christ, who was shooting? Bullets zinged around him, his men dashed out with guns roaring, while the men with mules came out blasting with weapons of their own.

And then more men. Where the hell had they come from? Three on sleek horseback, and two from the rear.

Goddamn it. Oh, goddamn it. The Rowlan brothers. Brander's chest squeezed hard. It hurt. His chest hurt.

He raised his gun and aimed at the younger one, Harrison, the patched-up soldier who didn't see Brander behind the bushes. Harrison raised his gun at Wittmann. The deputy shot first, Harrison ducked from that blast as well as Brander's, but Harrison's bullet hit Wittmann in the chest. He flew off his horse and fell on some rocks. Stone dead.

Brander himself hadn't been shot, but his left arm crumpled with pain. What was it? First his chest, now his arm. One of his revolvers fell to his thigh and dropped to the ground. He kicked his horse with his spurs, it neighed—the damn thing—and tore off like thunder up the cliffs.

Gunfire started to fade, but the sound of hooves kept steady time behind him. A rider. Someone coming…after him…

He fought for breath. Heard the sound of his own gulping and heaving…wheezing…groaning…

Must try to reach…top of boulders…

His horse wouldn't cooperate. He dug the spurs in deeper…horse reared…he held on…torture on his heart, pounding through his cranium, gasping for air…kaleidoscope of colors swam before his eyes.

He toppled completely over the horse and his hip slammed against rock. The count of his heartbeat was off…skipped a beat…squeezed pain…skipped another…

A man stood above him.

"Brander. Put the gun down. Put the gun *down!*"

The pain blacked it out…. The sun's rays, the beautiful sun of Alaska, the one thing he adored about this land…stabbed his eyes with light.

"Brander…we can make this easy or we can make it hard."

Lifted his gun… The man…that god-awful outlaw in the Wanted poster, dove for safety.

The blast hit empty air…. Brander wept…. His heart lost its rhythm…. He clawed at his chest…. God have mercy…. He felt cold.

Autumn looked out her kitchen window for the tenth time that hour. Where was he? It was close to eight o'clock, eleven hours since Quinn had galloped out of town. Maybe he'd never come back.

"Don't fret," Victoria told her, gently tapping her elbow. "He can take care of himself. He always seems to land right-side-up. Please eat something. There's more stew left in the pot."

"I'm not hungry." Autumn soaped up the coffee cups in her bucket. *Please God let him come through.*

Victoria touched her hand again, and motioned to the window.

He was here!

Autumn swiped her hands against a tea towel and raced out to the street.

Quinn, bent over his horse, riding calmly alongside his brother, directed the other men with him—Vic, Ben, Trevor and Jackson, whose leg was bandaged—to stop outside the jailhouse. Autumn assessed the situation quickly as her heart pounded with the thrill of his return.

Not wounded. Moving slowly and deliberately, calling soft orders to his men, searching for and finding the two lawyers in the crowd. Where was Brander? Where were his ugly collection of hired guns and deputies?

A crowd was forming around the returning men. Gilbert arrived, panting from his run. Dear Gilbert, who'd risked his own life by cutting a key for Autumn, stepped up with the other men from her original posse. Champagne Charlie and his father came out of the hotel and joined the others. She couldn't hear what they were saying, but step by step she drew nearer.

She wasn't sure exactly when she left Victoria behind. Autumn focused on Quinn's dark face, the intensity of his expression, the powerful stance that squared off who he was and what he'd accomplished. She drowned out the oohs and aahs of the listening crowd to marvel at the man that Quinn Rowlan truly was.

With a light step, Quinn jumped up the boardwalk stairs outside the jailhouse and tore down his Wanted poster. His brother, Harrison, climbed up and, with a smile, tore his off, too. The other men followed, one by one.

It was a sight to behold, and Autumn knew there and then that it was over. The crowd cheered. Quinn, in the middle of it all, finally looked down the street fifty yards and saw her.

His gaze locked on hers. Time swirled around them as they made a steady pace toward each other. Every nerve ending in her body tingled.

"Quinn," someone shouted. "Tell us where his grave's at."

"Quinn," said another. "Will you take over? As deputy marshal?"

"It's not for me," he said softly, reaching her side. "But Jackson might be interested."

The crowd rushed to Jackson. Harrison tried to calm everyone, but Autumn could see how pleased his men were over the turn of events.

"You're free," Autumn whispered to Quinn. She stared up into his face.

His hat dipped close to his brow, his eyes deepened with pleasure as he looked at her and his cheeks pulled upward.

"I wanted to prove myself to you."

"You have."

Quinn's mouth took on a more sorrowful twist. "He's dead. We took his body to Dyea. Got some witnesses to record what occurred. Then we buried the dead. From the fourteen miners and their guards, three got wounded. Six of Brander's men were killed. Two are still alive and confessing to the rest of their crimes."

"I'm sorry about the wounded men." She ran a hand to her throat. "But you saved so many others."

He nodded. The brim of his hat slashed through the soft evening rays of the sun.

"Are you free for dinner?"

She smiled and her eyes watered and she laughed and nearly cried all at the same time.

Then she glanced down at her apron. "Give me a minute to change."

Disagreeing, he grabbed hold of her wrist, and playfully whisked her down the side street toward his hotel, out of view from the others. "You've never looked better."

"Your best suite, please," Quinn told the front-desk clerk. "Run a bath. And let me have a look at your menu."

It was hell for Quinn to wait. He wanted to be alone with Autumn. His heart rushed, beating in time with the clock on the wall.

Autumn stayed her distance, perhaps not wanting to appear too eager. In front of Quinn, or in front of the hotel staff? Quinn unfolded the menu on the pine counter and pushed it toward her so they could read together.

He placed his finger on an assortment of appetizers and main courses and bottles of wine. She nodded approval of everything. "But select what you like, Quinn," she whispered. "Don't order all of it."

"All of it," he said to the clerk.

The gangly young man tapped the bell and

pressed his spectacles farther up the bridge of his nose. He slid a key discreetly to Quinn.

"The lady here will be joining me for dinner only. Then I'll retire to the private suite on my own."

"As you say, sir."

Like hell. Quinn only wanted to protect her reputation, but he had other plans in mind.

Quinn gave her a look and she, raising her beautiful eyebrows with a tempting smile, went up the stairs ahead of him. He enjoyed watching her walk—the twist of her hips, the curve of her backside. He moaned and took a deep breath to pace himself. There were so many things to say.

When they reached the two-room suite, the staff had already opened the bedroom door. One clerk said they would be hauling boiling buckets of water from the downstairs boiler. Another one, a young woman, added scented salts to the bathtub.

In the dining room, two other staff members were preparing for a feast.

A knock on the opened door brought a delivery of champagne in a bucket of ice. "Courtesy of Champagne Charlie," the middle-aged clerk said. "For Mr. Quinn Rowlan."

"Thank you," said Quinn.

"Well, isn't he quick," said Autumn, but she smiled with approval.

In the half hour it took for them to complete the filling of the tub and stacking of towels, the food arrived. It sat steaming on the dinner table as Quinn led the last clerk out the door.

"Thank you. We'll call if we need you. Looks splendid." He tossed the man some coins for the staff.

The clerk bowed. Quinn left the door to the dining room propped open until he lost sight of the man. Then, when all was quiet on the top floor of the hotel, Quinn shut the door and locked the latch.

He turned around and approached the woman who drew him so completely. He traced the corner of her soft temple, ran a thumb along her jaw.

Take it slow, he thought. He wanted to savor every moment.

"You are a sight for sore eyes, darlin'."

"You're not too bad yourself. For a wanted man."

She looked from the loaded dinner table to the other room that held the steaming tub. "What are you going to do first? If you eat first, the water will get cold. If you bathe first, the food will."

"Thought I'd do both."

"Hmm?" Suddenly appearing nervous, she wrung her fingers into her skirts. Looking down at her apron, she frowned as though just remembering she was wearing it, then undid the ties at the back and slipped it to the settee. This left her in a navy skirt and clinging navy bodice. Her blond hair, sparkling in the stream of evening light coming through the window, framed her pretty eyes and cheeks. He could sit and stare at her for hours.

But his clothes were dirty from the trail and he

needed a good wash. He strode to the bathroom doorway and removed his holster. He dropped it gently to a table inside, where he could reach it. Not that he was expecting any more trouble, but more out of habit.

"How about you take a quick bath?" She motioned to the water, then the windows on the opposite corner of the suite. "I'll wait for you out here. There's a chair by the window—"

"Come here."

"I don't want to interfere with all you have going—"

"Come here."

"The staff will think it's peculiar—"

"Come here."

Still, she didn't budge. She lingered at the muslin curtains. Was she as disbelieving as he that they were finally together? That she was finally free to go about her own business matters in town? That the ordeal he'd gone through in the last two years that had required every ounce of his energy was finally over?

It thrilled him to the sky.

"Shy, Autumn?"

She shook her head, then stopped herself and stared at him across the room.

"I was hoping you'd meet me halfway. But looks like I'll have to take matters into my own hands. As usual." He pretended to be serious.

He strode up to her, wrapped his arms around her

middle, inhaled every breath of her skin and planted his lips softly on hers. It was like a dream. Then with a whoop of surprise from her, he lifted her off her feet, and they landed together on the cushioned bench by the window.

Chapter Twenty

Autumn looked up into Quinn's eyes, loving the look and feel of him pressed against her. This was it now. They were together. No more interference, just the two of them. She wanted to tell him all she felt, but knew there was time enough for everything. She savored the anticipation.

"I'm told I don't smell too good," he said apologetically.

She looked up lazily. "I don't care."

"Let me go soak in the tub." He rose and untangled himself from her grasp.

"Shy, Quinn?" she teased.

He didn't reply, but began to peel off his clothes. First his shirt, revealing a brown toned back with muscles she could watch for hours. He tossed the shirt to the Oriental rug, then took off a boot. Then another. Tossed those, too.

His belt came next, with its shiny brass buckle.

Her heart started to hammer in her throat for what was coming next.

She heard the sound of buttons unbuttoning, then he stepped out of his jeans. Pure masculine attraction. Bare white buttocks, muscled thighs and glorious brown yards of manly shoulders. And a Stetson.

"Coming, Autumn?" He'd reached the door of the bath and glanced over his shoulder. With a quick stride to the dinner table, he took the bottle of champagne and two flutes.

"I'll bring the appetizers." She bolted for the platters of deep-fried shrimp and pickled vegetables.

"You are the appetizer."

At the tub, he tossed his hat on a wall rung, swung around, one hundred percent gorgeous in his nakedness, and stepped into the scented water. It was murky, clouded white from the bath salts, but heavens, she could still get a good gander at his front as he slid in. Her eyes trailed down his breastbone, his firm chest, the light matting of hair that went lower and lower and lower….

He splashed water lightly in her face, breaking her spell. "I need someone to scrub my back."

"I could send a message to the front desk."

"You could. Or you could take this brush—" he handed her a pretty sea sponge tied to a handle "—and do me the honor."

He dipped his whole body underwater, including his head. He had to lift his knees—he could barely fit—and it made her giggle. Such a huge man. And that enchanting area of male seduction…

Up he came, gasping for breath.

She let him relax then fed him a shrimp. He took it from her fingers and gave her one in return. Then a piece of freshly baked bread, warm from the oven.

With a chunk of soap, he scrubbed his face, his neck, his shoulders, his armpits. There was something splendid about watching a man bathe. He propped one leg up on the edge of the tub, soaped it up, then the other.

"Turn around," he said, suddenly insisting on modesty.

She exhaled in a breath of contentment and did so till he was thoroughly washed.

He poured the champagne and they drank. It was bubbly in her nose and tasted deliciously sweet.

"I've never had any before."

"Champagne?"

"Mmm-hmm." He looped his fingers around her wrist and she wished he never had to let go.

"My back, miss, if you don't mind."

"My pleasure." She stepped to the rear of the tub and kneeled on the rug, behind its pewter claw feet. It was one of Champagne Charlie's special tubs that he'd imported from California. She recognized the shape as similar to one at the Imperial.

With scrub in hand, she gave Quinn's shoulders a firm rub. They were slicked from the water, smooth and hard. He moaned as she did her job. She wanted so badly to please him, to make him feel needed and adored, she concentrated on rubbing his muscles.

When she was nearly finished, she felt sure he was asleep, so quiet was the water and still was his body, but she couldn't see his face.

Then, as she laid the brush on the floor towel and took a minute behind him to watch the rivulets of water trailing down his shoulders, he whispered gruffly into the air. "I love you, Autumn."

Her hands stilled on her lap.

She inhaled the steamy air, was aware of the fragrance of the water, heard the drip of the water droplets from his fingers to the tub, could taste the lingering flavor of champagne on her tongue, and mostly, mostly, coveted the feel of being alive in her own skin. Of loving her moment with this man.

"Did you hear me?" he asked softly, still talking to the curtain.

"I did. I'm enjoying the sound of it."

"I love you, Autumn," he repeated. He seemed to revel in the words himself.

On her knees, she dipped around the side of the tub and kissed his bristly cheek. "I love you...love you...love you...Quinn Rowlan. Wanted in Alaska."

With a stirring of her heart, she waited as he searched her face for what seemed like an eternity. Then he snatched her up, picked her right up off the floor, onto his lap in the tub, and kissed her fully on the mouth.

Water sloshed to the carpet, over the rim of the tub to the platters of food, but they didn't care.

Breathless with need, Autumn kissed him back, loving the feel of his hot tongue searching for hers, his hand on her wet corset, the yanking of her blouse from its skirt. He unbuttoned the skirt and ripped it off her. She removed the wet blouse, the corset beneath, slid her wet stockings down her legs till she was sitting on his lap naked.

He glanced down at the tips of her breasts. They stood straight out, bumps of flesh so sensitive all he did was kiss one and the feeling went straight through her chest to her stomach.

"I've never seen anything so lovely…so remarkable… You're all I've ever wanted, Autumn. From the moment I laid eyes on you."

"Quinn…when we met…I felt as though you'd walked straight into a secret chamber of my heart. You just started talking…and talking."

"You were the only one listening. The only one who came up with a plan to cover for me in Skagway. Right under Brander's nose."

"When you told me you were a lawyer, I couldn't fathom what you'd been through. Couldn't believe a man would give it all up to keep facing the same monster again and again. You could have left at any time and gotten lost somewhere in the States."

"I was so lost…until I found you. Now it's over…it's over…."

He moved his tongue to her throat, to the back of her ear, all the while grasping her wet clumps of hair, as though her strands were ropes he could tie himself to and never let go.

He cupped the underside of her breasts, kissed her cleavage as her breasts swayed to his face, cupped both in one hand and kissed the nipples. She rode his stomach, at the same time feeling his erection between her buttocks. All she had to do was lift up slowly, and he could tuck himself inside.

"Autumn," he whispered against her temple. "I know it's early, but I have plans. Those plans include you in my life. I'd like to stay here in Skagway and build a home. I'd like to practice law as a prosecuting attorney for the District of Alaska. Do you think…think you would like to be a part of that?"

She kissed him feverishly on the cheekbone, the temple, his eyebrow. "I'll be with you anytime you say."

"What I mean is, darlin', I'd like us to marry. I'd like you to be my wife. Would you have me?"

Speechless, she pulled away, her breasts grazing his chest. She adored the steamy feel of hot water in contrast to the cool air on her nipples. His hands gripped each cheek of her behind, and it struck her how humorous their position was as this gentle and dangerous man was proposing marriage.

"You listen to everyone who crosses your path. You weigh every story for its truth. You'll make a remarkable prosecutor. I'm proud of you."

"And?" He waited, breathless.

She wiggled her behind toward his erection, and he got the message.

"I'll take that as a yes." With a glint of trouble—trouble she wouldn't mind taking on—he spanned her rib cage with his huge hands and pulled her close for another slow kiss.

Quinn couldn't get enough of the wench. And she'd agreed to be his wife. With a sigh of admiration and delight, he lifted her off his lap and sat her back against the back of the tub.

"Ah," she said softly, as though disappointed, "I thought you were going to plant me squarely on your lap."

"Oh, I plan on doing just that. Something else first."

He rose on his knees before her, lifted one of her luscious thighs to the edge of the tub and kissed her foot. It must've tickled, for she wiggled her toes and squirmed. He loved that about her. Her ability to enjoy every sensation.

He kissed up her calf and up her thigh, and then suckled on her breast. Her bosom was striking. The two plums he'd remembered from the night they'd spent together on the trail bounced and jiggled before him. He could barely fill his mouth.

When he moved his lips lower to her stomach, he felt her shudder beneath his tongue. He cupped her rear end and lifted her gently to kiss her in her middle. She grew suddenly still and he understood that no man had ever kissed her there before.

The pleasure was all his. It made him rock hard and ready.

Kissing her feverishly there, over and over with his tongue, nibbling on the delicacy till she was on the brink, Quinn could think of no other place on earth he'd rather be. She pulled his head away and gasped.

A slow smile spread over him, rooted itself in his gut where it would always stay. She closed her knees and glanced at his body as though in love with every inch.

Then suddenly she was on her knees, nibbling on the tip of his shaft, circling that hot luscious tongue around the edges, working her way downward with her mouth. He thought he would burst with the need to come.

Just before he could, he broke free and sank back against the porcelain.

"Now," he said. He pulled her closer and helped her sit on his lap.

He deliberately avoided contact with her private area, preferring she wait it out till she was good and ready.

Seemed she was. She nibbled on his throat and he cupped one swaying breast, then tugged her nipples. She bit his lower lip. He bit the corner of hers.

With a firm hold on her buttocks, he gently slid her derriere toward his shaft, lifted her slightly up and out, and slid inside.

A hot pocket between the two of them. Her breath grew feverish, her eyes glistened and she eased herself up and down as though testing how much he could fill her.

He filled her plenty. She was tight and hot and his.

As they joined together, drawn in a mist of love and champagne and the finest food to be bought in Alaska, this time as they made love, he came inside the woman he cherished.

"Still hungry?" Autumn, dressed only in the fluffy robe the hotel had provided for Quinn, sat across from him at the dining table. It was getting late. They'd drawn the curtains and had created a golden nest of warmth and colors. Lanterns and candles flickered around them.

She lifted a spicy chicken drumstick to her mouth. Her robe drifted open to reveal her bouncing breasts. She felt the cool air waft over her saturated skin. When she saw his eyes drift over, she knew he was riveted, and she enjoyed the pleasure he received from her body. Her heart hammered. Quinn could always stir her emotions.

He leaned back on his chair, eating like a hungry mountain lion. He was dressed only in a towel, naked from the waist up. His gaze lingered on hers, his brown eyes flecking with soft bits of green.

"Promise me when we marry," he said, sipping on another glass of champagne, "you'll walk around naked all the time."

Her stomach rippled with her smile. "All the time,

Quinn? Won't that be difficult if you're trying to study your papers?"

He filled her glass. The bubbles curled up and up and up, like miniature floating balloons.

"Not difficult at all. Promise me if I ever get too serious about something, you'll take off your blouse and show me what's what."

He searched her face. She was feeling lazy and wanton and all she really wanted to do was kiss him everywhere, all over again. The muscles in his dark chest flickered with the light of the candle behind him.

She laughed softly. "I promise."

He dipped his bread in a bowl of jam and licked the juices off his fingers. Even his appetite made her want him more, sexually. It was beyond her, how much two people could share when they were in love.

"Although it might be *you* who has to distract *me* sometimes." She cupped a spoonful of rice into her mouth and wondered if he'd be surprised at her news. "If *I'm* too businesslike."

He lifted his champagne for another sip but stopped halfway to his lips. With his hair still damp, he looked youthful and adventurous.

"What do you mean?"

"With the extra money I'm collecting from liquor sales, I'm able to put some away."

He dropped one hand to his chest, brushing it down his stomach. Lord, she was riveted by his golden skin.

"What are you planning?" he asked.

"I spoke with Champagne Charlie. Nothing's set yet, but he agreed to talk about my plans. I'd like to open my own little shop in the hotel." She watched as Quinn's face perked up in animated surprise.

"I'd like to call it the Lady's Shop. Nothing too large, just a little spot to call my own, really. A place to sell my knickknacks and little clocks. Bolts of precious fabrics that are hard to find elsewhere. Journals and recipe books and women's magazines I collect from the ships that come in."

"You are something."

She beamed with pride. "The way I've planned it, I figure I may be able to invest in a property of my own next spring. And if I save for another year or two, there may be no need for a banker at all."

He dangled a long, muscled leg over the edge of his chair and looped it up on the rung of hers. Connected in as many ways as possible, he was eager to hear more.

"Mary, the owner of the sandwich shop, told me how steady her income is, and how to hire help so the shop is open twenty-four hours. With all this daylight, someone's always awake and wanting to shop. Anne the jeweler agreed to help me with some of the pricing. If I ask, maybe Champagne Charlie would like to sell some of his bathtubs—"

"Not without a cut to you."

He was such a man, wasn't he? Her future husband. Always looking out for her.

"Yes, of course." She rambled on with enthusiasm.

She could talk for hours on the subject of business. "In the boardinghouse above us, you should see...old Mr. Sawyer makes these soft rag rugs that any woman would love to have beneath her feet."

Autumn scooped another spoonful of rice onto his plate, aware he was studying her, even though she could barely stop for a breath between thoughts. "Did you know Miss Flora is a painter? Watercolors. They're magnificent. Tiny little landscape paintings of Skagway. Miniatures. Maybe if I approach her..."

"Autumn, you're going to be a huge success."

It was lovely to be able to talk to him about her plans, a man who was interested in her life and what she wanted from it.

He nodded softly in approval. She leaned against the back of her chair and draped a hand over the slats. Her robe slid against her naked, silky skin. She watched his gaze lower to the spot.

"What's Harrison going to do?"

"Says he's staying in Alaska. With me."

It would be wonderful to get to know her new brother-in-law. Family she never had.

"Quinn, I think about the evening we first met. Beyond the costumes, I was masquerading as a singer, pretending to be content with the way my life was going. And you, in your masquerade, were supposedly a vicious criminal. You turned out to be the most just man of all."

She rose from her chair, stepped over to his and

hugged him. When he nuzzled his face to her parted robe, she knew with a delighted sigh she was in for a long night. He'd do anything in the world to help her. Just knowing that…was what made her future so appealing.

* * * * *

Author's Note

$\curvearrowright$

Alaska has a fascinating history. Many considered it to be the last Western frontier of the nineteenth century. It was swarmed by tens of thousands of people during the Klondike Gold Rush. Law and order took a while to catch up, so many con artists made their way north. One man in particular stands out. Jefferson Randolph Smith. His nickname was "Soapy."

Skagway, in the District of Alaska, was the major disembarking port for gold miners heading over the mountains to the Klondike. Gold was discovered in 1896 on a tributary of the Klondike River in the Yukon Territory, Canada.

Smith was an organized-crime leader who ruled the town of Skagway and made life hell for folks on the trail. He bribed, killed and stole his way to notoriety. In July of 1898, he was gunned down in the streets. It turned out he had many apparently legitimate people on his payroll, including the deputy marshal.

Although the deputy marshal in my novel is fictitious, he was inspired by true history.

Harlequin is 60 years old, and Harlequin Blaze
is celebrating!
After all, a lot can happen in 60 years,
or 60 minutes…or 60 seconds!

Find out what's going down in Blaze's
heart-stopping new miniseries,
FROM 0 TO 60!
Getting from "Hello" to "How was it?"
can happen fast….

Here's a sneak peek of the first book,
A LONG, HARD RIDE
by Alison Kent.
Available March 2009.

"IS THAT FOR ME?" Trey asked.

Cardin Worth cocked her head to the side and considered how much better the day already seemed. "Good morning to you, too."

When she didn't hold out the second cup of coffee for him to take, he came closer. She sipped from her heavy white mug, hiding her grin and her giddy rush of nerves behind it.

But when he stopped in front of her, she made the mistake of lowering her gaze from his face to the exposed strip of his chest. It was either give him his cup of coffee or bury her nose against him and breathe in. She remembered so clearly how he smelled. How he tasted.

She gave him his coffee.

After taking a quick gulp, he smiled and said, "Good morning, Cardin. I hope the floor wasn't too hard for you."

The hardness of the floor hadn't been the problem. She shook her head. "Are you kidding? I slept like a baby, swaddled in my sleeping bag."

"In my sleeping bag, you mean."

If he wanted to get technical, yeah. "Thanks for the loaner. It made sleeping on the floor almost bearable." As had the warmth of his spooned body, she thought, then quickly changed the subject. "I saw you have a loaf of bread and some eggs. Would you like me to cook breakfast?"

He lowered his coffee mug slowly, his gaze as warm as the sun on her shoulders, as the ceramic heating her hands. "I didn't bring you out here to wait on me."

"You didn't bring me out here at all. I volunteered to come."

"To help me get ready for the race. Not to serve me."

"It's just breakfast, Trey. And coffee." Even if last night it had been more. Even if the way he was looking at her made her want to climb back into that sleeping bag. "I work much better when my stomach's not growling. I thought it might be the same for you."

"It is, but I'll cook. You made the coffee."

"That's because I can't work at all without caffeine."

"If I'd known that, I would've put on a pot as soon I got up."

"What time *did* you get up?" Judging by the sun's position, she swore it couldn't be any later than seven now. And, yeah, they'd agreed to start working at six.

"Maybe four?" he guessed, giving her a lazy smile.

"But it was almost two…" She let the sentence dangle, finishing the thought privately. She was quite sure he knew exactly what time they'd finally fallen asleep after he'd made love to her.

The question facing her now was where did this relationship—if you could even call it *that*—go from here?

* * * * *

Cardin and Trey are about to find out that
great sex is only the beginning....
Don't miss the fireworks!
Get ready for
A LONG, HARD RIDE
by Alison Kent
Available March 2009,
wherever Blaze books are sold.

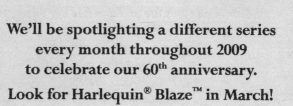

REQUEST YOUR FREE BOOKS!

Harlequin® Historical
Historical Romantic Adventure!

2 FREE NOVELS PLUS 2 FREE GIFTS!

YES! Please send me 2 FREE Harlequin® Historical novels and my 2 FREE gifts (gifts are worth about $10). After receiving them, if I don't wish to receive any more books, I can return the shipping statement marked "cancel". If I don't cancel, I will receive 6 brand-new novels every month and be billed just $4.94 per book in the U.S. or $5.49 per book in Canada, plus 25¢ shipping and handling per book and applicable taxes, if any*. That's a savings of 20% off the cover price! I understand that accepting the 2 free books and gifts places me under no obligation to buy anything. I can always return a shipment and cancel at any time. Even if I never buy another book, the two free books and gifts are mine to keep forever.

246 HDN ERUM 349 HDN ERUA

Name	(PLEASE PRINT)	
Address		Apt. #
City	State/Prov.	Zip/Postal Code

Signature (if under 18, a parent or guardian must sign)

Mail to the **Harlequin Reader Service:**
IN U.S.A.: P.O. Box 1867, Buffalo, NY 14240-1867
IN CANADA: P.O. Box 609, Fort Erie, Ontario L2A 5X3

Not valid to current subscribers of Harlequin Historical books.

Want to try two free books from another line?
Call 1-800-873-8635 or visit www.morefreebooks.com.

* Terms and prices subject to change without notice. N.Y. residents add applicable sales tax. Canadian residents will be charged applicable provincial taxes and GST. Offer not valid in Quebec. This offer is limited to one order per household. All orders subject to approval. Credit or debit balances in a customer's account(s) may be offset by any other outstanding balance owed by or to the customer. Please allow 4 to 6 weeks for delivery. Offer available while quantities last.

Your Privacy: Harlequin Books is committed to protecting your privacy. Our Privacy Policy is available online at www.eHarlequin.com or upon request from the Reader Service. From time to time we make our lists of customers available to reputable third parties who may have a product or service of interest to you. If you would prefer we not share your name and address, please check here. ☐

HH08R

You're invited to join our Tell Harlequin Reader Panel!

By joining our new reader panel you will:

- Receive Harlequin® books—they are FREE and yours to keep with no obligation to purchase anything!
- Participate in fun online surveys
- Exchange opinions and ideas with women just like you
- Have a say in our new book ideas and help us publish the best in women's fiction

In addition, you will have a chance to win great prizes and receive special gifts! See Web site for details. Some conditions apply. Space is limited.

To join, visit us at
www.TellHarlequin.com.

THBPA0108